PICTURE IMPERFECT

By the Author

Amigas y Amor Series

Little White Lie

Under Her Skin

Picture Imperfect

PICTURE IMPERFECT

by

Lea Santos

2010

PICTURE IMPERFECT

© 2010 By Lea Santos. All Rights Reserved.

ISBN 10: 1-60282-180-1
ISBN 13: 978-1-60282-180-4

This Trade Paperback Original Is Published By
Bold Strokes Books, Inc.
P.O. Box 249
Valley Falls, NY 12185

First Edition: September 2010

Credits
Editor: Stacia Seaman
Production Design: Stacia Seaman
Cover Design by Sheri (graphicartist2020@hotmail.com)

Acknowledgments

Thanks to all the readers. You make the magic happen.

Dedication

For my best friend, Terri. Love you!

CHAPTER ONE

From Paloma Vargas's journal, Saturday, September 1

I don't know if Iris's impending commitment ceremony is pushing me to this point, or if I'm just tired of feeling like an orphaned wife. But I can't take it anymore.

Deanne forgot our anniversary.

Again.

And, thanks to the ever-available excuse of a "work obligation," she wasn't here to wish the boys well on their first morning of school. Considering it's Teddy's first year of all-day school, well, I can't tell you how it hurt to see the disappointment on his little face when his mommy didn't show. Pobrecito.

Not to mention Deanne and I still haven't made love...

Damn. Fourteen years of love I've given to that woman. If you count the time we dated, we've been together more than half my life. (Scary.) I have never loved a woman other than Deanne Vargas. I always will—she's our boys' mommy, too. But I need more than a wife and so-called breadwinner. I need a lover and a best friend. If that makes me selfish, so be it.

I wish I could figure out when things changed and go back. Make things turn out differently. But I can't, any more than I can go on living like this. A woman's gotta do what a woman's gotta do, no matter how terrifying. And I've never been more scared in my life.

Thunder rolled, and fat angry raindrops slapped the windows of Paloma and Deanne's west Denver home. The dreary slate-colored sky gave the impression of day's end, though it was only a few minutes after four o'clock. Paloma set aside her journal and released a long sigh, her eyes fixed on the water-blurred grayness outside. *Just perfect.* The day might not be over, but a long chapter in her life was. The dismal weather seemed to reinforce the awful, inevitable step she needed to take.

One hot tear slid down her cheek, and she smacked it away, determined to discourage any of its followers. She rarely cried. No sense blubbering now. Standing, she crossed to the antique iron bed and resumed her awful task, folding the last of her wife's clothes and placing them into the suitcase.

She glanced down, fingering the cream-colored note card with their vows printed on it:

**Sometimes when we say
"I love you," we forget it *isn't* a simple thing
or a sentiment we can take for granted.
As we join hands, hearts, and lives, may we always remember
where we've come from to reach our "I love yous,"
how lucky we are to be here now, and exactly where we're headed
in order to whisper more of them against each other's skin, always.
May we forever cherish the you…and the me…and the us.**

Jesus. If this was being cherished, Paloma would hate to experience being taken for granted. So help her God, this was the last damn time Deanne would bring storms to her life or pain to her heart—

"Mama?" Pep blinked at her from the doorway, his perplexed gaze ping-ponging from the open suitcase to her undoubtedly ravaged face. Hesitant, Pep stood on one tennis shoe–clad foot, the second shoe resting atop the first. Flour dusted the Denver Broncos T-shirt that was almost too small for him. His innocent eight-year-old face was smeared with the chocolate he'd been using to make cookies with his little brother. "Are you leavin'?"

Pain unlike anything she'd ever felt shot through her.

The *us* had become far more than Deanne and her alone.

Their sons.

Dear God, their *sons*.

Paloma wobbled toward Pep and knelt, pulling him against her until she could feel his heartbeat on her face. She might have told herself she was trying to comfort Pep with the gesture, but the opposite was closer to the truth. His warm little-man body made her feel like, somehow, she would find the strength to get through this horrible task of ending the marriage she'd thought would last forever.

"No, *m'ijo*. I'm not going anywhere. Mommy—" Paloma's words caught, and her heart pounded a funeral dirge. How could she explain a failed marriage to the boys when she'd hardly grasped it herself? Would they understand without hating her, blaming her?

"I'm staying right here with you and Teddy. But Mommy has to…go on a trip," she finished, clearing her throat. A trip to Get-A-Clue Land, where absentee moms and wives realized they couldn't continually put their families last or they'd find themselves alone.

Knowing that everyone assumed she and Deanne had the perfect life hurt almost as much as admitting to herself that the so-called high school sweetheart, fairy-tale romance was finished. Hell, Deanne had barely touched her for…she didn't even know how long.

Sigh.

Okay, she did know.

Six months, one week, three days, and—she checked her watch—four hours.

Lesbian bed death in a big way.

Paloma knew because she'd written it down, along with every other important detail in her life. Keeping journals as she had since she'd been a young girl was a double-edged sword. Yes, she had a chronology of the good times, the memories, the milestones. But lately, every time she reread the entries from the past few years, she also faced the black-and-white reminder of all that her fraud of a marriage lacked.

> *Deanne missed dinner tonight and didn't call. I was worried.*
>
> *Deanne forgot Pep's birthday party today. Pep cried.*
>
> *Deanne forgot our anniversary. Again. Fuck it. I don't care anymore.*

Paloma fought the urge to sob. Perfect life? Ha! As long as she could remember, she'd been the one to accommodate, to compromise, to make things better. *Smile and the world smiles with you.* Damn, she was sick to death of it.

Now, if not making love for six months was the only rock on their marriage path, she could maneuver around that. She certainly wasn't so shallow that she'd give up a fourteen-year commitment over six sexless months. But, if she were completely honest, things had started changing when Pep was born.

Yeah. Pep was eight.

The lack of physical intimacy was clearly a symptom of a much larger underlying rift. It wasn't that Deanne treated her badly or abused her in any way. She had simply forgotten Paloma existed, which was, frankly, a deal breaker. One Paloma couldn't overcome. Whoever said apathy was worse than hate was a damned smart cookie.

"When's Mommy comin' back?"

Pep's plaintive question yanked Paloma back to reality. She blinked several times, unsure how to answer. "I don't know, baby." She smiled tenderly. "Where's Teddy?"

"Downstairs watchin' cartoons," Pep said about his six-year-old brother. "We're ready for the oven. We did all the dough balls on the cookie sheet."

"Good boy." Paloma ruffled his soft crew cut, a style both he and Teddy wore and loved. "Any problems?"

"Nuh-uh." He scratched his chin, where some melted chocolate had dried and cracked. "Teddy dropped a few chunks of dough on the floor, but he picked 'em up and ate 'em, so the floor is still clean."

Paloma cringed at the mental image of how her kitchen probably looked right now. That, and the fact that her son had been scarfing raw cookie dough straight off the floor. But, what the hell. She'd mopped the day before. The boys couldn't do permanent damage to themselves or to the kitchen by spooning cookie dough onto a sheet—or eating it off the floor, for that matter. Besides, she had desperately needed the time alone to think.

And pack.

Letting them do the cookie prep had been the perfect solution.

Paloma took Pep's hand and stood. "Come on. After the cookies are done and you yard monkeys take baths, I'm driving you over to spend the night with Aunties Emie and Gia." Emie Jaramillo wasn't a blood relative, but she, Paloma, and Iris Lujan, the third musketeer in their little band of pals, had been the best of friends since high school. As far as Pep and Teddy were concerned, Iris and Emie—and now the women in their lives, Torien and Gia, respectively—were *familia*. And Paloma couldn't agree more. "How's that sound?"

"Cool!" Pep brightened. He loved his Auntie Gia, due in part to Gia's big, rumbly black truck. Paloma's sons were hard-core vehicle freaks. *Just like their mommy.*

As though a fresh and amazing idea had popped into his head, Pep sucked in an excited breath. "Can I—?"

"Yes, beetle bug." Paloma chuckled, answering patiently. "I'm sure if you ask politely you can sit in Auntie Gia's truck."

Pep's face lifted into a mask of amazement. "How'd you know I was gonna ask that?"

"I'm your mama, little man." She bent and kissed him on the head, then smacked him lightly on the rump. "I know everything."

They started down the stairs. "But…you don't know when Mommy's comin' home, do you?" Pep's little voice sounded searingly grave and much too wise to the reality of the modern family.

Make that broken family.

Damn, Pep was only eight years old. Teddy, just six. *This is going to be sheer hell.*

"Hello!" Paloma called out before shutting the unlocked front door and entering Emie's and Gia's house in Washington Park. She stomped the rain off her shoes onto the mat and peered around the lamplit hallway. The house felt so warm and welcoming, as opposed to her home, which lately had seemed about as inviting as a body bag. Pep and Teddy, toting sacks of oven-warm cookies, took off at a run to find their favorite truck-owning auntie.

"Don't run, boys! Your shoes are wet." They continued unheeded, and Paloma didn't have the energy to scold them.

"We're in here," called Emie from the vicinity of the kitchen.

Muffled laughter danced through the house, waltzing with the aroma of fresh coffee. Iris and Torien were also there. Happy couples whiling away a bad weather Saturday together. Probably discussing Iris and Torien's impending commitment ceremony in P-town, something Paloma didn't think she could stomach discussing at this point.

Maybe I should've called first.

She sighed, feeling so out of the loop. For the longest time, she and Deanne were the only ones living in happy coupledom. Now Emie and Gia were expecting their first baby in November— something Emie had always wanted and never thought she'd have. Iris and Torien were so much in love, it literally hurt to look at them. Paloma was the consummate fifth wheel.

The divorcee.

The failure.

Soon, anyway.

She set the boys' overnight bags aside, then shrugged listlessly out of her raincoat and shook it over the mat before hanging it on the bent wood hall tree. For the first time in her life, she didn't look forward to seeing her friends. She dreaded their shock when they learned she was leaving Deanne. *Leaving Deanne.* So surreal.

"There you are."

Paloma spun around, hand on her chest. Beautiful Iris, who had recently retired from her long, successful modeling career, peered around the corner of the living room, luminous green eyes smiling down at her. Considering the foot of height difference between five-eleven Iris and Paloma, Iris always smiled *down* at her.

"You scared me," Paloma breathed, her voice too airy, too brittle. *Oh, God.* She was teetering on the brink.

Iris tilted her head in curiosity. "What's taking you so long, girl? You forget the way to Emie's kitchen?"

"No. I just…I was…" Paloma's nose burned, her throat ached, her muscles sagged, heavy and inept. She'd managed to stave off every potential crying bout since she'd made peace with her decision, but right now, she had the overwhelming urge to fling herself face down on the floor and bawl like a baby. But she was a grown woman and a mother.

Soon to be a single mother.

Don't cry. Don't cry. Don't cry.

Unable to stop the torrent of pain, Paloma slumped onto the bottom step of the staircase and surrendered to the tears.

"Pea? Jesus, what on earth is wrong?" Alarmed, Iris squatted in front of her. "Did you have a car accident?"

Paloma shook her head.

"PMS?"

"No. I'm sorry. I shouldn't c-cry." Paloma felt the comfort of her friend's arms encircle her. Resting her face on Iris's shoulder, she reached up and smeared at the tears blurring her vision in time to see a very pregnant Emie waddling into the hall.

Emie stopped short and nudged up her fashionable new eyeglass frames. "What happened?" Fear laced her voice.

"I can't believe it has c-c-come to this," Paloma slurred.

"Mama?" ventured Teddy's tiny, quavering voice. All three women glanced toward where he stood tentatively in the archway to the living room. "What happened to my mama?" Tears cracked his words, his eyes round and serious. His little chest heaved with frightened breaths.

"Oh, *hijito*, it's okay," Iris soothed, beckoning him over. "Your mama just…"

"Stubbed her toe," Emie blurted, "and she's being a big whiny baby. That's all."

Teddy glanced from Emie, to Iris, to his mama, questions in his troubled eyes. "Mama? You have an owie?"

She struggled to give him a reassuring smile. "I'm okay, baby. It doesn't hurt much."

God, how it hurts.

"Want me to kiss it?" he asked in a solemn tone.

Paloma sniffed loudly and held out her arms for her big, brave boy. She didn't know what she'd do without these kids. "Come here, you. Kiss me, instead."

Teddy scampered into his mother's arms, and she showered his face with tear-moistened kisses. He settled onto her lap, nestling his head in the crook of her neck. She could smell his wind-whipped little boy scent and the chocolate chip cookies on his breath. It didn't surprise her they'd dug in already, and really, what did it matter? The cookies would spoil their dinner, but no more than finding out their mama and mommy weren't going to live together anymore.

"See?" Iris tucked a lock of long black hair behind her ear and flashed him a Colgate smile. "Mama's all better."

"Mama looked like she was gonna cry earlier when she was packin' all of Mommy's clothes up, too," said Pep, who had just come into the hallway. His tone was matter-of-fact, far too wise for such a little guy.

"Pep," Paloma chastised, softly.

Blotches of red stung his cheeks, and he darted glances at the adults before hanging his head. "Well, you did."

Paloma cast a furtive peek at Iris and Emie before lowering her gaze to the floor as well. Leave it to Pep to bust her in front of her friends.

After a moment, Emie leaned into the living room, bracing her lower back with a fist. "Gia?" she called. She turned a falsely bright face to the boys. "You guys want to go outside with your other aunties and look at the truck?"

"Nah. We'll stay here with my mama," Pep said, ever protective.

"Yeah," Teddy chimed, snuggling closer to Paloma's warmth.

Gia's sculpted form darkened the archway, and one glimpse of the smoldering, love-wrought look she exchanged with Emie caused Paloma's tears to come anew. Paloma remembered the heated glances Deanne had given her when she was pregnant, brimming with pride and excitement over the children they would raise together.

Those were the good days, the memories that made the stark reality of today so goddamned unbearable. Now, when Deanne spared a glance in Paloma's direction at all, she seemed to look right through her. Clearly, Deanne wasn't attracted to Paloma anymore—that much was obvious. Granted, Paloma did weigh twenty pounds more than she had when they'd fallen in love, but she'd also given birth to two freaking sons. Didn't that earn her the leeway of a few extra curves?

Maybe she repulsed Deanne.

Maybe Deanne would be thrilled to know Paloma wanted out.

Maybe this whole thing was some cruel twist of destiny.

She sniffled against Teddy's soft hair.

"¿Qué pasó?" Gia asked Emie, her worried gaze on Paloma. She reached back and pulled her sleek black mane into a ponytail, securing it with the spare band that always seemed to be on her wrist when it wasn't in her hair.

"Ah, Paloma stubbed her, uh, toe." Emie's words were light, but she told Gia so much more with her eyes. "Can you take the boys outside while Iris and I tend to her?" Iris, meanwhile, spoke in low, urgent Spanish to Torien, who nodded with understanding.

Gia grabbed Pep around the neck. "Did one of you guys kick your mother in the toe?"

Pep laughed and squirmed. "No, Auntie Gia. Stop."

Gia moved toward Paloma and scooped up the younger boy as well. "Come on, Teddy my man. Let's go outside."

"It's rainin'," Teddy reminded them, in a tone that clearly said he thought the grown women in the house were more than a little dense.

Gia looked momentarily stumped.

Torien stepped forward. "I need some things from the garden store. Perhaps you boys would like to come along?"

Gia set Teddy and Pep down in the archway. "Great idea. And I happen to know there's an ice cream shop right next to your Auntie Toro's favorite garden store."

As always, Gia had the magic touch with the boys. They bounced and clapped their hands at the prospect of yet more sugar.

"Not too much," Paloma said, her voice dispirited and wan. "They just had cookies."

"We all did, and they were great," Gia said, patting her flat abdomen. "But Mama's the boss. Just two scoops instead of three, guys."

"Gia," Emie scolded, playfully.

Gia gave Emie a quick air kiss, then winked.

Teddy took Auntie Torien's hand and grinned way up at her. Pep followed suit, entwining his fingers with Auntie Gia's. In a wave of excited little-boy chatter and a cacophony of footfalls, they headed toward the back of the house where Gia always parked her truck.

Paloma stared unseeing at the gleaming hardwood floor until she heard the back door slam. The house fell silent but for the tick of the grandfather clock Gia's mentor, Mr. Fuentes, had given her and Emie as a housewarming gift.

Paloma released a long breath and wished she could fall asleep there.

Wake up later and find out it had all been a bad dream.

"Talk, Pea," Iris said gently.

Paloma hated that she'd broken down, especially in front of her sons. She didn't even know how to start. "I'm fat," she mumbled. "I'm fat and ugly."

"Hey," Iris said, settling cross-legged on the floor in front of Paloma. "Stop that. You are neither fat nor ugly, and what does that superficial bullshit have to do with anything anyway?"

"Iris's right." Emie indicated the distended middle of her normally pixie-thin figure. "Besides, *this* right here is what you'd call fat."

Paloma rolled her eyes. "You're pregnant, Em. That doesn't count. But the point is, I'm through."

Iris and Emie waited for more.

Paloma gulped back her misery. She tucked her naturally curly hair behind her ears and felt the wet ends drip against her upper back. "I packed Deanne's stuff today." The grandfather clock chimed once; to Paloma it sounded like the punctuation at the end of a sentence.

Divorced.

Period.

"That much we got, thanks to Pep fronting you, as little boys will. And?" Emie prompted.

"And I'm asking her to leave." Paloma swallowed. She squeezed her eyes closed. "For good."

Emie and Iris remained hold-your-breath silent so long, Paloma finally opened her eyes and searched their faces for some reaction. "Did you hear me?"

"Oh, honey, yes. We did, but—" Emie said, the expression in her intelligent brown eyes sincerely distraught. She moved closer and smoothed her hand over Paloma's hair. "That's such a big step. Maybe you just need some time apart to work things out."

"No. I'm tired of trying to keep things together. I'm killing myself to make life perfect for everyone but *me*, and it isn't even working." A short laugh devoid of any bit of humor escaped Paloma's lips. "Trust me, it's over."

Silence.

Clock ticks.

Sadness.

"God, Pea. I don't know what to say," Emie whispered.

"Me, neither," Iris added. "You and Dee have always been, like…the perfect couple."

Paloma ran her hands over her chilled upper arms. Her now-dry eyes stung from all the crying. "You know, what the hell? Truth is, Deanne left me long ago. She just forgot to take her physical presence along. I'm just finalizing the split."

"Wow. I had…no idea." Emie cleared her throat. "I mean, have you two talked about it?"

Paloma shook her head, slowly, exhausted from the misery. "Not really. We stopped talking a long time ago, too. Lovely when the sordid truth comes out, huh?"

"Pea," Iris said, reaching out to hold Paloma's hands. "I'm so sorry. But I do understand. Yes, we knew you'd been unhappy, even with you putting on a happy face. Trust me, that much was clear."

Startled, Paloma blinked. "And here I thought I'd been hiding it well."

"We know you better than that," Iris said. "We've known you forever."

"True." A pause. "That's both cool and it sucks."

"When will you tell her?" asked Emie, absentmindedly stroking the mound of her baby-swollen belly.

"When she gets home from work tonight, whenever the hell that is." Paloma gestured to the matching duffel bags slumped against the hall closet door, and her chin quivered. "I brought overnight bags for the boys, if that's okay. I don't want them to hear—"

"Of course," Emie said. "Don't give it another thought."

A mournful silence ensued. Paloma leaned her head against the newel post on the stairway. "You know what yesterday was?"

Emie's eyes widened and she furrowed her fingers into the new spiky-pixie hairstyle that perfectly complemented her gamine features. "No, sorry. I'm pregnant. I can't remember my own name at this point."

Iris sucked in a breath. "Damn Deanne," she muttered, anger brightening her cheeks.

Paloma nodded, her tone flat. Defeated. "Yep. August thirty-first. Our fourteenth anniversary. And it passed just like any other unimportant day."

"Oh, Paloma," Emie said on an exhale. "I'm so, so sorry."

"Yeah, me, too," Paloma said, her resolve returning. "But, trust me, it'll never happen again."

Dee Vargas heaved her black canvas work bag into the trunk of her prized Chevelle and waved good-bye to a couple of shift-mates in the fenced parking lot of the Denver Police District Four substation on Clay Street. The rain-dampened cement lent a chalky, raw smell to the air and washed her skin in goose bumps. She reached for a wadded jean jacket and shrugged into it, her motions slowed by exhaustion. Swing shift had been slammed with calls right out of the chute and straight until end of watch. Bar fights, domestics, traffic altercations—why couldn't people get along these days?

She shut the trunk, then lowered herself into the driver's seat of the pristine restored 1970 muscle car. *Off duty, at last.* She closed her eyes. God, she was tired. All this overtime might be padding their family savings and making her look good for the upcoming sergeants' promotion, but damn. It was killing her. She just wanted to go home and veg out.

Good luck with that goal.

An elusive but distracting presence in the form of unspoken tension seemed to have invaded their home life like an occupying force. Paloma had withdrawn into a dangerous kind of quiet in the past...Jesus, had it been a year already? More? They never fought, but it was as if Paloma gently boiled just below the surface. Never having had a good role model as far as committed relationships were concerned, Dee figured she'd best just shut up until it blew over—whatever *it* was.

Dee moved uncomfortably through the motions of living, always feeling like she'd made some grave misstep where her wife was concerned. Small talk didn't work, because Paloma didn't go for it. Neither did sex, if Dee even remembered correctly. She didn't dare initiate sex when Paloma's GO AWAY vibes flashed so incredibly strong. Instead, Dee threw herself into work, hoping the extra household money would melt the ice that had seemed to form around Paloma's heart where their relationship was concerned.

God, she didn't know what else to do.

The thought of facing that radiating tension made Dee hesitate to turn the key in the ignition, and that made her one hell of a shitty partner. But why wasn't Paloma the affectionate, easygoing woman Deanne used to know? Instead, Paloma remained polite, in a tight-lipped, conspicuously silent kind of way that made Dee's heart pound with trepidation.

Because *something* was wrong.

Something was horribly wrong.

What had changed?

Dee should ask. She knew that. But right now she just didn't have the energy—and the plain truth? The idea of hearing the answer terrified her. She remembered feeling exactly like this around her mother, so afraid of hearing verbal confirmation that Mom was unhappy with her for this particular transgression or that one. So she'd walk on eggshells whenever she sensed something was wrong with Mom. Staying out of sight, deflecting verbal blows, and hoping to God things would get back to normal. As a coping mechanism, it wasn't the best. But she didn't know anything else, and it had always worked. Eventually Mom would transform magically back to her old self, and Dee would breathe a sigh of relief.

Waiting out the storm, however, wasn't working as well with Paloma.

It wasn't working at all.

It had to be Dee; that was the rub.

Something she'd done.

Said.

Something she hadn't.

Try as she might, she couldn't figure out what on earth had gone awry. She worked hard—damn hard—and took care of Paloma and their sons in the only way she knew how. She grabbed as much off-duty work as she could find. Sure, Dee hadn't told Paloma she was up for a promotion because it was still a gamble, and the thought of dealing with more of Paloma's disappointment, as well as her own, if it didn't happen was too much to bear on top of everything else. Plus, Dee rationalized, if she did get the promotion, maybe the pleasant surprise would bridge the mysterious chasm that had cracked between her and Paloma, repair the marriage she valued so…*damn*…so much.

Rationalizing, Dee.

She blew out a sigh. Who knew anymore? Who *ever* knew?

Fatigued to the marrow of her bones, she dragged a palm down her face. Bottom line was, she loved her wife and sons with her whole heart and soul, with an intensity that shook her to the core. She loved her career, too, and it gave her great pride to provide a good life for their family. But lately, everything seemed to have spiraled out of her control and she couldn't get a hand hold—which wasn't her standard *modus operandi*. Surely nothing serious…

Fellow officer Joe Gann rapped on Dee's window, startling her from her glum thoughts. Dee glanced over, and Gann motioned for her to roll it down.

Dee did. "What's up, Gann?"

"You okay?"

"Just tired," Deanne told him.

"I hear that." The tall, loose-limbed redhead jerked his thumb in the direction of an idling green Pathfinder carrying several of their other shift-mates. "We're headin' to Lucero's for a few beers. You comin'?"

The damp night chill swirled into Dee's car and mingled with the fresh scent of the vinyl polish she'd rubbed into the dashboard the previous day. Hands wrapped around the steering wheel, she considered the invitation. Beer, wings, and mindless cop banter. Dee knew she should say no, but the stress of Paloma's disconcerting demeanor made a no-pressure beer with her coworkers sound damned inviting. Really, what could it hurt?

Dee rapped her thumbs against the wheel—*ba-da-bum*. "You know, that sounds good," Dee told Joe. "I'll follow you."

❖

Paloma woke with a start when she heard Deanne's key in the lock. Her neck had stiffened while she'd dozed in the chair, and she winced as she straightened and stretched out the kinks. Paloma glanced at the anniversary clock on the mantel.

Two hours late.

Big surprise.

So much for hashing things out.

It was past one a.m., and now Paloma just wanted Deanne to leave.

The front door opened and bonked into the suitcases Paloma had left in the foyer, which she could see from where she sat. Her heart thrummed. She heard the scrape of the heavy bags against the tile, followed by Deanne's mumbled expletive.

D-day.

Paloma stood and crossed the room on wobbly legs, her gaze focused on the packed luggage, her throat unbearably tight. A strip of blue moonlight reached like an ominous tentacle into the otherwise dark hallway.

Paloma watched, filled with tingly trepidation, as Deanne peered around the door. That same bluish light deepened Deanne's short black hair and played light and shadow on the curve of her jaw, her regal cheekbone.

Deanne's breath caught at the exact moment she noticed the suitcases, and time froze.

Suddenly dizzy, Paloma gripped the edge of the wall.

Deanne flicked on the hall light, and her baffled gaze sought and found Paloma's face, eyes troubled, cautious. "P?"

Muscling past the obstacles into the hall, Deanne stopped. She clutched a grocery store bouquet of flowers—red roses, pink carnations, and white daisies. The bouquet hung limply against her muscular thigh, forgotten.

How fucking symbolic.

Paloma couldn't take her eyes off the blossoms, and eventually Deanne followed her line of scrutiny.

As though she'd just realized they were in her hand, Deanne tentatively held them out to her. "Baby, I…I know I forgot our anniversary yesterday, and I'm so so…God, I've had so much on my mind, but that's no excu—"

"It doesn't matter," Paloma said. "Just…set them down."

Deanne looked so crushed and contrite as she placed them carefully atop one of the suitcases, Paloma almost felt guilty.

Almost.

She lifted her chin and pushed away the twinges. Goddamnit, she had borne all the forgotten events, the disappointments, the unwanted changes in their relationship without a single word of complaint, just like she'd been raised to do. But she couldn't placate Deanne any longer.

Contrition or not, Paloma had reached her breaking point.

"It does matter." Deanne spread her arms then let them fall to her sides. "I know it does. I'm so sorry, Punkybean. I shouldn't be so busy."

Paloma huffed, denying how her stomach swirled hearing that oh-so-familiar voice form the silly pet name Deanne been calling her since she was fifteen years old and addicted to designer jelly beans. Paloma's gaze fell to the baggage, and her mind to the emotional valley between her and this woman she'd loved for… *Jesus*, for so long. She couldn't look at Deanne. At her familiar strong shoulders, at her brown, smooth skin. Frankly, Paloma couldn't look at Dee at all, at least, not without knives of pain slicing through her. Deanne was a beautiful woman. A beautiful person. But somewhere along the line, they'd splintered.

Such a loss, this marriage.

Such a goddamned loss.

"I'm sorry, too," Paloma said, choking on the words. "Believe me."

The night air from the open door billowed the hem of Paloma's ankle-length robe.

Deanne's hesitance loomed long and thick.

Paloma forced herself to look at her wife, just as Deanne glanced, again, at the baggage between them.

"Are you...going somewhere?" Deanne's expression remained guarded.

Silence. Thick and pain-laced and beyond awful.

"No." The weight of fourteen years of commitment settled on Paloma's shoulders. "You are." Her voice came out shaky, and she fought to steady it, squeezing her hands together in a painful knot.

This wouldn't get any easier.

Just say it, Paloma.

"The boys and I are staying here, in the house they're used to. They need the stability." They both held their breath through a stony pause. "You're leaving."

Deanne's brows dipped and her jaw slackened. She started forward but stopped when Paloma stepped back. "What are you talking about?" Deanne's question sounded husky, incredulous. Bewildered and hurt.

Having blurted the most difficult words, Paloma's emotions tumbled down like the house of cards this relationship had become. She ached, she nearly keened, but no way in hell would she cry. She wrapped her arms around her middle, dug her fingers into the sides of her waist. "Damn you, Deanne. *Damn* you. I've loved you more than half my life. But I can't handle being treated like a nobody any longer. No—it's more than not being able to handle it. I *won't*. I deserve more than that, and so do the boys."

Unstoppable this time, Deanne advanced on her until Paloma could see rain droplets glistening on her hair and skin. Back pressed against the wall, Paloma turned her face away from

Dee's nearness and closed her eyes. "A nobody? You think I treat you like a nobody?"

Deanne gently pulled Paloma's chin around and waited until Paloma looked at into her eyes. "Really? This is me, baby girl. You and me. How could you think—?"

"Stop." Paloma pushed Deanne's hand away, an inhale pulling in the familiar pine, leather, and night-air essence of Deanne, despite Paloma's attempt *not* to smell it. "Seriously… just stop. I have tried as much as I can, compromised as much as I'm willing to." Tears threatened. "This is killing me, Dee, can't you see that? But I have to do what I have to do for me." She held a breath. "It's…it's over." Paloma skirted past Deanne and retreated a few steps into the dark living room, as though the shadows would cloak her in safety.

Deanne stood utterly still, horror and disbelief blanching her face as she clearly tried to grasp—or deny—the meaning of Paloma's words. "What? What's over?"

"Us! You and me, D. The farce our marriage has become."

Realization transformed Deanne's features into something Paloma would never push from her mind, no matter how hard she tried.

"No, Paloma. Please. Don't say—"

"Damnit! Listen to me. *Hear* me. For once, I need you to—"

"I'm right here," Deanne said, her tone soothing. "I want to hear you. Every word."

Paloma clenched her hands, shoring her resolve. "I can't continue playing the role of happily ever after when everything's so wrong between us. It has to…end."

Unshed tears sprung to Deanne's widened eyes. Her chest rose and fell with harsh breaths. "So, that's it? Just like that, you blindside me? For God's sake, if things have gone so unbelievably wrong, why haven't we talked about it?"

Silence.

"We can make this better." She moved toward Paloma and

gripped her arms with desperate intensity. "It's always been you and me, Punky. How can you say it's over, like it never meant a thing? How?"

"I have to do this. Don't act like you didn't see this coming," Paloma said, her voice raw.

"But that's the thing. I didn't see it." Her thumbs moved in circles on Paloma's arms. "Clearly, we're out of sync, but in my mind, we're destined to be together, beyond everything."

Silence.

Deanne pushed out a frustrated sound. "You never told me anything was wrong."

"Seriously? I shouldn't have *had* to tell you. If we're so damn destined to be together, you should've seen. You should've known. You should've *tried*, for God's sake." Paloma shook off Deanne's hold and, again, moved away. Gripping the edge of the door, Paloma turned and set her jaw. "P-please, I don't want to run this thing in circles. Just...go."

Deanne gaped as if Paloma had lost her mind. "Are you fucking kidding me? I won't 'just go.' This is our *family* we're talking about. If there are problems, we'll fix them. If I've done something wrong, I'll make up for it. I won't give up—"

"Listen. I don't have the energy to argue, and I'm not kidding," Paloma said, losing her steam. "You should have been home hours ago. We could've talked then. But I'm exhausted and I'm so angry I'm shaking. I don't want to talk to you now. Go, please. At least respect my wishes enough to give me some time and space."

Deanne stared at Paloma from the living room, the shadows carving deep hollows in her tear-moistened cheeks. Her throat moved over a wave of soul-deep pain. With a sharp exhale, at last, she snatched up the suitcases.

"You win, Paloma. I'll leave. For tonight." Grim determination tightened the skin around her eyes. "But this is *not* over. We are not 'over.' Not by any stretch of the imagination. You," Deanne said, her voice cracking, "you are my wife."

CHAPTER TWO

Written on Deanne Vargas's crumpled cocktail napkin from dinner, Wednesday, September 5.

TO DO:
Wash and wax car
Laundry
~~Look for apartment~~
Ask Ruben if I can stay a little longer
Talk to Paloma about the kids. About everything
Punkybean. Why?

For the millionth time since she'd stormed out of her home a few days earlier, Dee lay wide-eyed on her brother Ruben's lumpy hide-a-bed and asked herself why she hadn't done more to change Paloma's mind that night. Why she hadn't argued more.

Pleaded more.

Apologized more. Until she was hoarse.

Why she hadn't cried, bargained, refused.

But she hadn't. Period. Instead, angered or dumbfounded by Paloma's demands—Dee wasn't sure which—she'd gathered the suitcases Paloma had packed, brushing aside the wilted bouquet that was, admittedly, a pathetic gesture of apology for a missed anniversary, and left.

She'd fucking *left*.

Ruben welcomed her to stay without asking questions, which was just what Deanne needed. She still hadn't told her brother what was up, and Ruben knew enough about Deanne's private personality not to probe.

Now, here Dee lay, unable to sleep without the familiar rhythm of Paloma's breathing beside her and knowing she didn't want to go on breathing herself if the only woman she'd ever loved was no longer in her life.

She threw a forearm over her eyes and tried to rid her mind of that awful picture of Paloma, her back pressed against the wall, peering up like a cornered doe on day one of deer season. Her dusky skin flushed with anger, disillusionment spiking the thick lashes into wet points around her huge brown eyes.

Dee had wanted to comb her fingers through Paloma's sleep-tossed auburn curls and kiss the trembles from her full lips. But she hadn't. Though her mind reared up with disbelief at Paloma's words, every nonverbal cue told Deanne that Paloma was beyond being convinced.

How could I have screwed up so badly?

With a vicious exhale, Dee turned to the side, punched the red-headed stepchild of a pillow she'd been sentenced to use, and tried to get comfortable, a futile pursuit. The metal support bar beneath the thin mattress cut into her thigh like a dull sword, and the basement felt dank and miserable. No offense to her brother, but it just wasn't home.

She glanced at the illuminated red digits of the borrowed alarm clock and scowled at the late hour. But, Jesus Christ, her wife had kicked her to the curb. Sleep was about last on her priority list.

As a young woman, Deanne had sworn she would be a better parent and partner than her father had been to her mother. Victor Vargas had callously left his wife with five young kids to support. Because of him, Mom had to work three jobs just to make ends meet. Dear ol' Dad had always valued "a good time" more than he'd valued his own family.

Good time Victor.

Life of the party.

Just one more beer…

None of it had slipped by Deanne's quiet observation.

Watching Mom drag home late at night, bone weary from working, working, working, had fired young Deanne's determination. Mom had never complained. Not once. But that hadn't mattered; in fact, it hardened the steel of Deanne's resolve. She vowed that when she committed to a partner, she would do everything in her power to show her wife how much she cared by working extra hard. She'd be the kind of provider her father had never even considered being, and she'd take care of Mom, too.

And that's exactly what Deanne had done—worked so hard she barely had a spare moment to think. Now Mom was enjoying her retirement, Paloma was able to be a full-time mother to Pep and Teddy as she'd wanted, all on Deanne's salary and extra-duty income. It had never mattered that Dee had no free time, that she often missed social events to work overtime, that she had to schedule in sex…when she scheduled it in at all. She had proven that sometimes the apple *does* fall far from the tree, and that was worth every bit of sacrifice. Deanne might have shared the man's blood, but she was nothing, absolutely *nothing* like Victor Vargas.

She'd been proud of that until a few days ago.

Why hadn't it worked? Why had all her back-breaking efforts only succeeded in driving her wife and family away? More importantly, what could she do about it? Because no matter what it took, Deanne would not lose Paloma and the boys to some failure she couldn't even wrap her brain around. God help her, she couldn't bear to consider it.

❖

"This is absurd," Paloma groused at Emie as they powerwalked through Washington Park the next morning. Emie had recently begun a sabbatical from the private university where she was a genetics researcher and professor, so she could devote a full year to her and Gia's first baby. Since Deanne had left a few days earlier, Emie and Paloma had met every morning after the boys were off to school to get their sweat on. Iris joined them when she could, though her impending commitment ceremony plans and work kept her very busy.

"What's absurd?"

Paloma wiped her forehead with her sleeve. "*You* are seven months pregnant, yet I'm doing ninety-nine percent of the huffing and puffing."

Emie swung her lean arms in the exaggerated but controlled manner she'd learned during a recent powerwalking seminar. A quick chuckle pulled dimples into her fine-boned cheeks. "It's your short legs. Plus, I've been doing it longer." She gave Paloma an encouraging smile. "You'll get used to it."

This particular morning, the park teemed with walkers, runners, and in-line skaters, thanks to summer's lovely weather hanging on with the tenacity of a pit bull terrier. As she struggled to regulate her breathing and keep the stinging sweat from her eyes, Paloma bucked the trend and wished the days would cool off.

She sighed and mirrored Emie's arm motions, if a bit awkwardly. The weird swishy movements were hard to get used to. "Well, I hope all this effort pays off somehow, because it sucks." She hadn't been so out of breath since...well, frankly, since—*damn*.

Unwelcome thoughts of making love with Deanne intruded into her unprepared imagination. Her stomach lifted, tightened. In her mind's eye, she saw herself in her lithe high school body, though, not in this rounder, older, birthed-two-boys form in which Deanne had shown zippo interest for months.

Or had it been years?

Her chest tingled. If the "no pain, no gain" credo held merit, she should be in Olympic form soon, because, God knew, she hurt, and not entirely due to the exercise.

Why, Dee? Why?

They used to be so in sync, so absorbed, so in love. The first six years of their marriage had been carefree and idyllic. Passionate, too. Big time. Give them a flat surface and a modicum of privacy, and they were all over each other. Horizontal, vertical—it didn't matter.

Then Pep came along, and that intensity began to shift, so gradually that Paloma hardly noticed. When she compared now with then, though, the difference in their relationship was drastic. *Why* it had changed was what Paloma couldn't quite figure out. Deanne had wanted the boys as much as she had. For God's sake, Dee had implanted her own eggs in Paloma's womb with detailed instructions from a midwife. The egg harvesting had been pretty strenuous and painful, but Dee wanted parts of both of them in the boys. After each implantation, they'd made love and cried—both times unbearably beautiful.

Were the relationship changes Paloma's fault? Had she accidentally gone from lover to mama, leaving Deanne in the lurch? Had Deanne fallen out of lust, then out of love, then into resigned complacency, like so many couples these days?

"Hurry up, slowpoke. What's up?"

Paloma bit her lip, and stepped up her pace. "Sorry."

"What are you thinking about?"

The pause lasted just a touch too long, and Emie would catch it. Still, Paloma opted for the evasive answer. "Nothing important."

Emie stopped and turned toward Paloma, grasping her shoulders. "Pea," she said, almost roughly, "it's okay to think about your wife. Don't lie to me."

"I-I'm not."

Emie huffed, but not unkindly. "Be real. I'm your best friend."

Paloma studied Emie's worried expression before admitting defeat. "Okay, fine. I was thinking about her."

"Naturally. She's the biggest part of your life, next to the boys, and it's only been a few days. Nothing's resolved. What did you expect?"

"I don't know."

Emie squeezed her arms, then released them. "Give yourself time."

Paloma bit her lip. "She hasn't even tried to talk me out of this."

Emie's eyes widened. "Hang on. You want that?"

"Well...no." A tight pause. "I don't know. I guess I'm completely petty and it just stings my ego that she hasn't even tried."

"Pea." Emie softened her tone. "You told Deanne to respect your wishes and leave. She left."

"That she did."

"Was it just a high school game? A ploy to get Deanne to beg for your forgiveness?"

"Of course not. I...meant it," Paloma finished weakly.

Emie cocked her head to the side. "And surely Deanne knows you wouldn't bluff about something so serious. That you wouldn't play games when it comes to your family. She's probably still reeling."

Paloma fought back the guilt.

"You did ask her for time and space, you know."

Paloma grimaced. "You aren't making me feel better."

"I'm sorry." Emie gave her a quick hug, then held her at arm's length and studied her. Without another word, Emie steered her to a bench dappled green and gold with sunlight through the fluttering leaves of the towering maple above. They sat.

"Okay, spill. I could use a break anyway." Emie rubbed the side of her abdomen, where the Amazing Kickboxing Baby, as she'd been dubbed, had been battering her for days. "Let's establish a few facts."

"You're such a scientist."

"Just shut up and answer. You still love Deanne."

It wasn't a question, really. No sense lying. "Yeah, of course. She's...everything. But so what? It takes more than just love."

"True. But love is a great basis. It makes almost every obstacle surmountable."

"Not this one." Paloma leaned over and plucked a dandelion, twirling it absentmindedly between her thumb and forefinger. The tubular stem felt both sticky and hollow, much like her life. "I feel like a failure." Embarrassment warmed her cheeks.

"It takes two to make a marriage work and two to make it fail. Don't shoulder the whole burden."

Paloma pondered this imponderable. "Do you know... before Dee left, we hadn't made love in more than six months?" It shamed her to say it, but maybe the first step toward recovery was admitting how tragically wrong things had gone.

Emie startled, but capped it quickly. "Seriously? Why not?" She dug through her knapsack for two bottles of water, handing one to Paloma, who set it aside.

"I don't know. The honeymoon was truly over, I guess. And the idiotic thing is, I could handle that kind of sexual apathy from another woman, I think, but not from Deanne." She lifted the dandelion beneath her chin and turned toward Emie. "Remember when we used to do this as kids, Em? If the yellow reflected on our skin, the girl-of-the-week was hot for us?"

"Pea, cut it out."

Paloma leaned forward. "It's not reflected anymore, is it? Look." Her voice cracked on the demand.

Emie reached out and gripped Paloma's wrist. "Don't do this."

"Why not?" Paloma pulled her wrist free and threw the dandelion aside, desperation welling inside her. "The girl is definitely not hot for me. I just don't know why not."

Exasperation reddened Emie's cheeks. "For God's sake, that's a silly kid's game. Whatever the problems in your physical relationship, they have nothing to do with dandelions *or* with your sex appeal." Emie raised a finger. "And don't bother denying that's what you're implying."

"Then what? If not that, what else could it have been?"

"I don't know. Sexual desire ebbs and flows."

Paloma huffed. "Apparently ours just ebbs."

Emie chewed the inside of one cheek. "Did you initiate?"

"I used to. All the time. One look at Deanne, and I wanted her right that second." A *long* time ago, her mind said. Paloma crossed one foot over the opposite knee and fiddled with her shoelaces. "But not lately, I guess." She liked to tell herself she'd stopped taking sexual charge when Deanne's attention seemed to wane, because who wants to face a string of rejections? But what came first? The proverbial chicken or the egg?

"Did you still want her that way, before—?"

"Yes. God, yes." Deanne Vargas was well and truly the love of her life. Other women simply didn't blip on her radar. "But I don't know if it showed. At least not…at the end." Ugh. It sounded so final. *The end.* "I was just, I don't know, so angry. So hurt."

"Well, what did Deanne say when you two talked about that?"

"I didn't really…ever bring it up."

"What?" Emie said, stunned.

"Deanne wasn't having sex either, you know." Paloma pouted. "She should have known something was wrong. She should have asked. She could've brought it up."

Emie released a humorless bark of a laugh. "Honey, I hate to break this to you, but women—wives, especially—have a lot of really useful skills, but mind reading isn't on that illustrious list. You have to communicate to make a relationship work."

"I know. Look, it's too late. I tried to wait out this…rocky patch, but to be honest, things started to change back when Pep was born. I've grinned like the perfect, supportive partner and mom for way too long. I have to stand up for myself this time."

Emie lifted her hands in surrender. "Hey, I support you. I just want you to be happy. But I won't lie—I can't picture you with anyone but Deanne."

"Neither can I." Poisonous worry burned in Paloma's stomach. In truth, she and Deanne had gone from fine, to silent, to separated, without so much as one fight. Was *that* Paloma's transgression? That she'd said nothing, that she'd allowed resentment to build, that she'd held everything in until the only word she knew to say was…good-bye?

"Hey, chicadees." Iris flashed her ubiquitous cover girl smile as she loped across the path toward them, a bundle of exuberance and joy and long limbs.

"Hi, Iris," Emie said.

Paloma merely smiled. She'd never seen Iris as content as she'd been since she'd fallen in love with Torien and left modeling to start a nonprofit with her. Iris might have the looks for the runway, but she had the heart for good works. The serenity of having found her true station in life showed in her every movement. She positively glowed. Paloma envied Iris that.

"I'm glad I didn't miss you guys completely." Iris wound her long hair into a spiky knot, securing a band over it, then said, "Scoot a cheek," to Paloma and sat down as soon as Paloma had obeyed. "What kind of exercise is this, slackers? Sit and Be Fit?" She still hadn't caught on to the aura of gloom that surrounded them like a gray mosquito net.

"No." Paloma leveled a bleak gaze at her. "We're trying to figure out why Deanne and I hadn't had sex in more than six months before the split. And, before that, why things had been getting progressively worse for—"

"Eight years, she says," Emie interjected. "Since Pep was born."

Iris's eyes darkened. "Really? That long, Pea?"

"I mean, it didn't happen instantly, but yeah." Paloma shrugged one shoulder. "I couldn't seem to powerwalk and explore that lovely topic at the same time. So we sat."

Iris wrapped Paloma in a side hug. "I didn't know. I'm sorry I was being so flippant."

"You weren't. You were just being you, which I love. You don't have to tiptoe on eggshells around me just because my life is shit." Impatience blasted through Paloma, directed at herself. "As a matter of fact, I'm tired of this 'poor me' tune I've been whistling. Know what I need? Hot and heavy no-strings sex. Wild, sweaty, boot-knockin' with a woman who can make me feel like a wanton, lusty—"

"Pea!"

"—slut."

Paloma met Iris's horrified gaze directly. "What? I'm serious. Hey—set me up with Tori's little sister. She's gorgeous. Definitely boot-knock-able."

"Uh"—Iris smacked Paloma's left thigh—"you're still married, dumbass."

"Separated," Paloma corrected her. "Big difference."

"*¡Cállate!*" Emie thwacked Paloma's right upper arm. "Madeira was in elementary school when we graduated, for God's sake."

"So?" Paloma jammed her arms crossed. "She's all grown up now, and not a stranger to the concept of a one-night stand, from what I've heard. Knocking a piece off of a hottie like Madeira Pacias would do wonders for my self-image and—"

"I'll tell you what'll do wonders for your self-image," Iris interrupted. "Spending some quality time with yourself. And I'm not talking about sex—although, go there if you gotta—but when it comes to Madeira or anyone else, drag your mind out of the gutter and listen."

"And please," Emie added, looking ill, "never use the phrase 'knocking a piece off' again. I can't think of you that way."

Paloma hoped her expression was appropriately skeptical.

Iris pressed on, undaunted. "Pea, this isn't about sex. Face it, you've always put yourself last. First in high school when

Deanne was Ms. Track Star and you basically supported her in that. Then college. Same deal—"

"Iris, she had a full-ride scholarship—"

"I know. I'm not judging. But you worked while she went to school, setting aside your own aspirations—"

"I wanted to do that. That was my choice."

"Granted, but you still put yourself last. And now, with the boys, you do it even more." Iris held up her palms. "I understand mothers have to make sacrifices, but you're a woman, too. You're Paloma. And somewhere along the line, you've forgotten that."

Iris had hit so close to the mark, Paloma squirmed and looked away. Her faults were agonizing in the light of day. Ugly.

"She's right," Emie said.

"You don't need to knock boots—"

"Stop!" Emie covered her ears.

"Or anything else with Madeira. Perish the thought—she's practically my little sister." Iris shivered. "What you need is some introspection."

What the fuck—sarcasm seemed as good a defense mechanism as any. "Intro*spection*?" Paloma scoffed. "And, that's ranked above sex on Maslow's Hierarchy of Needs? Since when?"

"Hush, girl." Iris squeezed her arm. "I'm saying you need to take stock of your future. You've made a major change. Now you have to figure out what to do with the rest of your life, where you want to be in five years. That's more important than scratching some sexual itch with a one-night stand."

Paloma looked down at her hands, which were clenched in her lap.

In five years?

Five years?

Pep would be—ugh—a teenager. A teenage boy from a broken home. Paloma hadn't imagined it that way, not in her wildest, worst nightmares.

She'd thought leaving her wife was the end, but her friends were dead-on right—as usual. It was more of a scary beginning. All she'd ever known was being Deanne's partner—her wife—and the boys' mother. Just like she'd always wanted. What else was there for her?

Cold apprehension clawed up her spine. "I wouldn't even know where to start," she admitted, her voice a rough whisper.

"All the more reason for you to do it," Emie said. "You've given yourself a clean slate, but Iris is right. Now you have to fill it. You have the boys, of course, but, God, Paloma, you're only thirty-two. What else do you want to write on that slate?"

Deanne.

The word popped into Paloma's mind before she could stop it. She squeezed her eyes shut, unable to imagine life without the woman she'd loved for so long. Yet her own actions, her request for a separation, had made living without Dee a stark reality.

Paloma wasn't happy in her marriage. Fact.

So why did the thought of ending it prompt such sparks of terror inside her? Flashes of fear? Aches of loss?

She had uttered the words.

She had set the wheels in motion.

She had better damn well get used to it.

And she'd better get used to herself—her new self.

She managed her first heartfelt, if a bit tremulous, smile of the day. "You're right. My life isn't defined within the parameters of being Deanne's wife anymore. A-and that's a good thing." She paused, drawing the corner of her lip into her mouth. "Right?"

"If you want it to be," Iris said.

Another pang of uncertainty struck, painful, like a snap against her flesh. "I just haven't gotten used to it yet. But I will."

"Atta girl," Emie said, beaming. "You'll get through this if you put your mind to it. You don't need Deanne."

Yes, I do. Jesus, I do.

"No," Paloma said sternly, hoping to quell the scared little scream building inside. "I don't."

❖

Dee stood on the curb and stared, dumbfounded, at the bucked hood of her patrol car, which was wedged up against the backside of the late-model Mercury Sable she'd corn-holed at the intersection. She took in the glass-strewn crash scene, the bent hubcap lying in a pool of power-steering fluid—an apt metaphor for the sorry state of her life.

Truthfully, Deanne's pride stung more than the airbag cut on her chin. She'd been en route to handle a nothing-special call. Her mind, of course, had been filled with thoughts of Paloma instead of focused on the job as it should have been.

When the Sable's driver braked instead of cruising through the yellow—exactly what most drivers did when a cop was behind them, a fact Deanne well knew—she hadn't given herself enough reaction time to stop. It was Police Driving 101, and her grade was a big, fat F. This was not an error an eleven-year veteran officer should make.

Yet, here she stood on Federal Boulevard, in the middle of the least cop-friendly neighborhood in her sector, while her supervisor, Sgt. Obermeyer, wrote the state report with Deanne's name printed in the at-fault box.

She pulled the four-by-four gauze patch away from her face, wincing when it tugged on the clotting blood. A glance at Obermeyer showed the sergeant engrossed in the paperwork, and guilt stabbed Deanne. Obermeyer hadn't shown any kind of emotion when she'd rolled on scene. Instead, she remained carefully neutral toward Deanne and her egregious mistake. Somehow, that felt worse than if Obermeyer had ripped her a new asshole.

As if reading Dee's thoughts, Nora Obermeyer glanced up

from the long state accident form, the breeze catching wisps of gray-shot blond hair that had escaped from her braid. "Grab the insurance card from the cruiser for me, Vargas."

Nodding once, Deanne started toward the car, then turned back. "Sarge, I'm sorry about this." To make matters worse, they were shorthanded to start with and Fridays were always busy. Now Dee had tied up not one but two cars with this mess.

"Now's not the time for apologies. We're slammed out there." Obermeyer glanced toward the tow truck that had just rumbled to a stop in front of the Sable. "Get the card, then go deal with the tow driver. Report to my office after this intersection is cleared and you've swapped out cars at shops. We'll discuss it then."

Deanne gave another stiff nod, then stalked toward the battered cruiser feeling glum and angry at herself. Obermeyer wouldn't yell; that wasn't the sergeant's style. But Dee could tell her longtime supervisor was disappointed by this lapse, and Dee couldn't blame her. First her marriage, now her formerly stellar job reputation. What next?

An hour later, Deanne rapped on the door to Sgt. Obermeyer's office, then entered, dread thick and sour in the pit of her stomach. "Am I interrupting?"

"No." Nora looked up from behind the battered metal desk, then stood. "Come in and have a seat. Actually, indulge me for a second. Come here." Nora walked around to the side of her desk.

Confused, Deanne approached her boss.

When the two were a couple feet apart, Nora leaned forward and sniffed. "Aha."

"What's going on?"

"A little intuitive experiment. My guess is, you're having problems with Paloma and it's affecting your judgment on the job." The statement confidently neutral. "That about hit the mark?"

Deanne stared at Nora, then bent her head and sniffed. Nothing. "Mind if I ask how you came to that conclusion?"

"I've been supervising officers for ten years, Dee. You for five. As your sergeant, and one who's trained to observe and catalog details"—Nora's eyes crinkled with wry humor—"but mostly as a woman myself, I happen to have noticed that Paloma uses a particular fabric softener on your uniforms. Gain—the same brand I use."

Deanne blinked. Twice. "I don't get it."

Nora shrugged. "Clearly, Paloma hasn't been the one washing your clothes, because that telltale fresh scent is history. Couple that with your uncharacteristic preoccupation of late, and it doesn't take rocket science to put it together."

No, but apparently it *did* take an astute sergeant like Nora Obermeyer.

The chair's dilapidated cushion wheezed as Nora settled into it, her gun belt squeaking with the motion. She adjusted her flashlight so it hung along the side of the chair, then steepled her fingers on the desktop. "I try to stay out of my officers' private lives. In light of today's incident, it's time you and I talk about your personal situation."

Deanne sank into one of the vinyl-covered swivel chairs that faced the desk, feeling dumbfounded and out of her league. For the most part, Obermeyer was just another cop, and a damned good one. But every once in a while, some odd thing reminded Dee she was also a woman, wife, and mother. So much like Paloma in so many ways. "Fabric softener? Seriously?"

"Well"—one of Nora's eyebrows quirked—"do you use it?"

Ridiculous that it hadn't crossed Deanne's mind to buy products *other* than the detergent, and truthfully…shamefully… Paloma had always done the shopping and washing, at least up until last week. Paloma had done *a lot* up until last week, come to think of it. Chagrined, confused, Deanne stared at her knees.

Should she seriously have known what laundry products Paloma used? Did her lack of attention to freaking fabric softener sheets contribute to Paloma's decision to kick her ass to the curb? For God's sake, she'd memorize every bottle, box, or can under the sink if she could just have Paloma back. She peered at her waiting sergeant, and her thoughts jerked back to her question. "Uh, no. I don't use it."

"My point exactly." Nora's hard gaze diffused into a look that bespoke of friendship more than rank. "Spill your guts, Dee. You aren't doing yourself any favors keeping it bottled up. As your friend, I care. As your supervisor, I need to determine if you can pull it together enough to work."

Deanne stiffened, her gut clenching. "I can work. Work's not a problem. It's my life. I just need…aw, hell." She scrubbed a palm over her face, then slumped back in the chair. "I need Paloma back."

Nora let the words hang in the air a moment. "She left?"

"Kicked me out."

"Were you cheating on her?"

Dee's head came up as if she'd heard gunfire. "What? Never." Her internal temperature spiked at the casually posed question. How could Nora think—?

"Any physical violence?"

Deanne strained forward, hot blood ripping through her temples. "Sergeant Obermeyer, I respect the hell out of you. You know that. But please don't insult me."

Nora didn't even blink. "No need to get angry. I'm not accusing you, but it's my duty to get a grasp of the basic picture, and these are standard questions IAD would ask, so…"

Teeth clenched, hands white-knuckled on the chair arms, Deanne said, "I would…*never* hurt Paloma or *any* woman."

Obermeyer didn't appear cowed or bothered by Deanne's vehemence. She nodded once. "Enough said." She flicked a hand. "Sit back, Vargas. Take a damn breath."

Deanne did. Grudgingly.

Nora crossed her arms. "Well, I'm all ears. I've been happily married to a civilian for twenty-six years and I've raised two sons and one daughter, none of whom use fabric softener, much to my chagrin." Her eyes crinkled with attractive crow's feet around the edges. "Maybe I can help."

Deanne willed her mind to knock down the fire of anger inside her. She took a moment to collect her scattered thoughts. Then, avoiding any mention of sex, which would have been way too uncomfortable, she haltingly described the rift of distance and silence that had split her and Paloma's marriage. Dee couldn't tell Nora how it started, or how it had gotten so bad, because she had no goddamn clue. She ended her tale of woe with the night Paloma had sent her packing with those damned suitcases.

When Dee finished, Nora's intuitive eyes were narrowed. She shifted in her chair, her weapon clanging on the metal armrest, then cleared her throat. "From what you've told me, her kicking you out doesn't make sense. You work hard, support the family. She stays home with the kids—which she wants, right?"

"Yes." At least, Deanne thought so.

Nora twisted her mouth. "Seriously, no arguments?"

Dee shook her head. "Paloma's never been confrontational. She never complains. She's great. Amazing."

Something in Nora's expression sparked. "Never complains. So, what about all the rest of the things married couples struggle with?"

"Such as?"

"Money? Child-rearing? Religion? In-laws?" A pause. "Intimacy."

Dee shrugged. "No problems. We've always seen eye-to-eye. We don't even bicker."

"Hmm." Nora drummed her fingers against her lips, searching for the elusive answer. Suddenly, the drumming stopped. "Were you attentive?"

"Attentive?" Meaning what?

The sergeant sighed. "Attentive, common spelling. Common

connotation. Did you give Paloma the attention she needed? You know, hugs and kisses, remembering her birthday and your anniversary. Did you bring her little gifts now and then just because you love her? That sort of thing. *Attentive.* It is a readily recognized word, Deanne."

With dismay, Dee recalled the pathetic grocery store apology flowers she'd attempted to give Paloma for having missed their anniversary. A twinge of guilt struck. She supposed she wasn't the most attentive partner on the planet, but it had never seemed to be a problem before. "Well, I...don't have the best memory for dates." Dee grimaced, feeling out of step and embarrassed. "But Paloma knows I love her. She wouldn't leave me over something so minor as forgetting an anniversary or two."

"Granted. I'm sure it was more than just that. But you're a woman yourself. You get this. Women want to feel loved and special. Remember"—Nora inclined her head—"Police 101: the crime is always based on the perception of the victim. It's what Paloma thinks that matters. What you think doesn't mean shit."

Deanne had never thought of her marriage in that way, as if she'd perpetrated some crime trying to...to what? To do the right thing? To not be Victor? Pain, like a hollow-point bullet, shot through her middle. Target: hit. She spread her arms wide in protest. "But the times I missed events or forgot special days, I was working."

"So fucking what?" Nora challenged. "Since when does that feeble excuse appease Paloma and the boys?"

Confusion smothered Deanne. Taking care of her family was a feeble excuse? "It didn't bother Paloma or she would've said something."

"You sure about that? I thought you said she never complained?"

Deanne pondered this. Dismissed it. Good point, but... "Paloma knew I was working *for her*, Nora. For the kids. To provide us a good life."

Nora leaned forward, her chair squeaking. "I get that. I'm sure Paloma does, too. But, because I'm pushy and you need the push, I would venture a guess she needed more, whether she verbalized it or not. Most spouses do."

Frustration squeezed Deanne's skull like the metal band on an electric chair. Truth be told, she didn't have that much experience with relationships. Paloma was her first…her one… her only. Her forever. "Like what? Paloma got to stay home to raise the kids, like she wanted. I provided for everything. She had security, freedom. Anything she needed."

"Except the one thing she probably wanted more than all of that. You." Obermeyer made a little gun with her hand and fired it at Deanne's heart.

Dee scowled, flicking away the words. "I told you. There's never been another woman besides Paloma. I love her."

"That's not what I meant. I'm talking about affection. Attention. Romance. Presence." Nora snapped her fingers. "Stick with me here."

"We—we had all that."

"Had?"

A sinking feeling in Deanne's heart dragged her gaze from Nora's too-perceptive face. "Well…then the boys came along, and I had to start thinking about their futures—"

Nora's tired laugh made Deanne feel like a child who didn't quite get it. "Damn, Vargas. I never knew you were so thick. No offense, but you sound like some of my male officers, and if you repeat those words, I'll deny ever having said them." A beat passed. "How'd you win her in the first place?"

Stung by the insult, Dee huffed. "Thanks a lot."

"No. Sincere question. You won Paloma once." Nora rolled her hand, urging some brainstorming. "How?"

What kind of whacko question was that? "Hell, I don't know. That was in *high school*. We were kids, not adults with a mortgage and two kids to raise, responsibilities."

Nor held up one finger. "But Paloma fell in love with you for a reason, true or false?"

Deanne paused. "True. I suppose."

"Okay." Nora inclined her head. "Find out why and how, and try to figure out when it ended."

Deanne had always been pragmatic. She didn't buy this right-brained, New Age relationship advice. It wouldn't solve a damn thing. She and Paloma couldn't be fifteen or eighteen or twenty-one forever. For Nora to suggest otherwise wasn't practical. The issue wasn't that Deanne had become a different woman. Or that Paloma had. The problem was, Paloma had kicked her out. Period. Why couldn't Nora stick with the matter at hand?

Frustrated, Deanne pushed to her feet and straightened her gig line, jutting her chin out to loosen the collar of her starched uniform shirt. "Thanks for listening, Sarge. I'll take your suggestions under advisement."

Nora followed Deanne's all-business lead and turned her attention to the stack of forms on her desk. "Good. Do so, Vargas. At *home*."

What? Horror riddled through Deanne. "You're suspending me for the accident?"

"Of course not. Accidents happen. Though I will have to note it in your critical incident file—just policy."

No surprises there. "Sure. But work is all I have now. About the time off—"

"Listen." Sgt. Obermeyer leveled Deanne with a clear blue gaze that left no room for argument. "You have a helluva lot of banked annual leave. Too much, frankly, which tells me you haven't seen the umbrella-drink side of a vacation in a long time. I strongly suggest you take one and get your shit together."

"But—"

"I'm not sentencing you to hard time, Dee, for God's sake. Do what the hell you need in order to get your life on track so your mind can focus on the job." Nora aimed her pointer finger at

Deanne. "You're no good to me in your current state. I don't want you here. It's not a suggestion, it's an order."

Deanne stood straighter. Obermeyer was right, which rankled. "Fine," she said, through clenched teeth. "How long?"

Nora shrugged, and tapped a pile of forms into neatly edged order. "It's up to you. The shift is fat, so we won't be short-handed. But be clear on one thing. I don't want you back here until your head's screwed on straight, and I'm talking, for good. If that means two months, it means two months. Is that clear?"

"Crystal."

"Good. Keep me up to date."

An awful thought rushed into Deanne's mind, and her stomach lurched. She cleared her throat. "How will, uh, this affect my chances on the sergeants' test? I'm on the list to take it mid-month."

Nora shook her head as though *Deanne* were the exasperating one. "Listen. You're an officer, not a superhero. It's okay—no, it's expected, actually—that you also have a *life*, and sometimes life gets messy. I guess it depends on how you handle it."

Another cryptic answer. "What I meant was, can I still come in and take the exam, even if I am on annual leave time?"

Nora sighed. "Yes. I'll note it, and they'll expect you there."

Deanne gave a curt nod and turned to leave.

"Hey," Obermeyer said, her tone softer.

Dee paused, hand strangling the doorknob. After a moment, she glanced back.

Sarge tapped the end of her pen on the desk a few times. "Think about what I told you when you're not so pissed off at me, okay? I'm only trying to help you save your marriage."

Heat rushed to Deanne's neck, but she held her supervisor's gaze.

"Consider it. That's all I ask." Though Nora's face remained serious, a whisper of a smile showed in her eyes. "And call me if you need to talk. Friend to friend."

Some of the tension eased around Deanne's mouth, but she knew she'd never call. "Thanks, Nora." *For a whole lot of nothing that makes any sense.*

CHAPTER THREE

From Paloma Vargas's journal, Monday, September 10

It's great being able to choose what I want to do with my life from here on out. But sometimes it feels like I'm searching for something to replace my marriage. No class or book or hobby can do that.

But wait. I don't want to think about Deanne.

DO-OVER.

What can I write about MY life? I started yoga classes over at the community college, and I've been to one session. Being around all those students got me thinking about going back to school. Why not? I didn't mind working while Deanne was getting her degree. We were always a team, and I did it willingly. To be honest, though, I did imagine I would get my chance later. (Damn, I brought up Deanne again.)

I called Torien, since she's working on a degree in Nonprofit Management down at Metro State, and we discussed different schools and courses of study. I think I'd like Metro. Torien says there are a lot of "non-traditional" students there (read: old), so I'd fit in!

Maybe I'll study English. I could be a teacher, or a writer. Or a book critic. (Ha ha.) Human Services looked interesting, too. I could counsel women to be more assertive. You know what they say: those who can't, teach.

I wish I knew what Deanne would think, but she probably wouldn't care. Wait. That's not fair. Deanne always cared. Man, I'm really contradicting myself. (And I brought up Deanne again, damnit.)

This...sucks. And if that's the only description I can come up with, maybe English isn't the degree for me. Okay, to hell with it. I'm going to bring up Deanne. I've never censored my journal entries before.

I can't get used to her conspicuous absence from the house. Sure, she wasn't home much before, but I could still feel her presence around, smell her shampoo lingering in the air. I could see (trip over) all the stuff she never picked up. Now it really feels like she's gone. I wasn't prepared. Not in the slightest.

Every day I think of things to share with her, then I remember. She's gone. My choice. Is it ever gonna get easier?

The boys miss her, too. Immensely. We've tried to be vague with them until we know what's gonna happen. We've explained that Mommy's just keeping Uncle Ruben company for a while because he's going through some grown-up stuff, but I can see in their innocent little eyes that they're worried. I don't want to keep Deanne from them. I don't want to keep them from their mommy.

Here I go placating again. Terminally happy Paloma trying to keep the world spinning. UGH! Best case scenario? I want life to be just the way it's always been for the boys, but different for me.

Me <————impossible dreamer.

I'm a mess.

A hot freaking mess.

The phone rang as Paloma was gathering her mat and water bottle for yoga class, stuffing it unceremoniously into the fuchsia bag she'd bought the day before. She scowled at the phone on the second ring. The boys had dawdled and bickered before school, and now she was running late. No time to chat. On ring three, she admitted defeat and tucked the receiver between her ear and shoulder while whipping harried glances around the room. Where'd she put that damn towel?

"Hello?"

"Ah, *mi hijita*. You sound distracted. It's a bad time?"

Her mother-in-law. Paloma froze, her stomach plunging like the proverbial baby grand from the thirty-first floor. She began to shake internally and couldn't stop. She hadn't expected Rosario's call so soon. Staggering to the nearest chair, Paloma sank into it, barely registering the pain when one of Teddy's pointy action figures gouged her thigh.

"Hi, Rosi." The false cheer in her tone made her cringe. "I was, uh…actually, yeah. Headed out. But I have a sec." She swallowed through a dread-tightened throat. "What's up?"

"No emergency, honey. You go on to your day."

No emergency? How'd she figure? "No. I have time for you." Paloma shot a glance at her watch and winced. She actually didn't have time, but she respected Rosario too much to blow her off, and this horrible, inevitable conversation had to happen sooner or later anyway.

"Just put my gorgeous daughter on," Rosario said, with laughter in her voice. "I'm planning the annual Broncos vs. Raiders family football party. I know you usually do all the scheduling, but you're busy. I can discuss it with Deanne. It's still a ways off. Go on."

The roar of pounding blood sounded in Paloma's ears.

Rosi doesn't know. Jesus, she doesn't have a clue.

The realization knocked the wind out of Paloma. She struggled for words, unsure whether to be relieved or completely fucking annoyed that Deanne hadn't told her mother about the separation. But…then again, she hadn't summoned the courage to call to her parents, either. She knew Mom would lecture her about her "duty" to fix things with Deanne, who was "such a good provider." All that hetero-based bullshit. Paloma loved her mother, but she couldn't stomach the "women make sacrifices, dear" speech again. It had been nearly two decades. Didn't Mom realize she and Deanne were *both* women?

"Paloma, honey? You still there?"

"Y-yes. Deanne's…uh"—*think, Paloma!*—"not…up yet," she finished, taking the coward's route. "C-can I have her call you?"

"Not up yet?" Rosario sounded surprised.

Okay, so yeah. It was the stupidest excuse she could have concocted. Deanne was a life-long early riser. Lying sucked. "Swing shift got off late, so she slept in for once and I haven't had the heart to wake her."

Rosario murmured a sound of approval. "You're a good wife to my daughter, Paloma. And a good mama. They're lucky to have you. We all are."

The room swayed before Paloma's eyes. She squeezed them shut and pinched the bridge of her nose until it hurt, Rosario's words warring with those of her own mother. The praise was undeserved.

A *good wife* didn't kick her partner out, now, did she?

A *good wife* worked things out, made things better, instead of letting them build and fester until they erupted into untold ugliness.

A *good wife* didn't lie to her mother-in-law.

What could she possibly say to this woman who had loved her and accepted her and Deanne's relationship from the very beginning? Who had championed it? Who had—for God's sake—given her daughter away to Paloma during their wedding?

The doorbell chimed, thankfully, saving her the trouble of commenting on Rosi's words. Paloma shot to her feet. "Hang on. Someone's at the door."

"Okay, honey."

She could've kept talking on the cordless phone while she traversed the room, but used the reprieve to collect her thoughts. She fumbled with the deadbolt, then yanked the door open.

Deanne.

Paloma's insides imploded. Not this, on top of everything else.

Dee held up one of Pep's textbooks, smiling, though the expression never quite reached her wary eyes. "I was in the neigh—"

Heart thudding, Paloma reached up and clapped a palm over Deanne's mouth. She feigned normalcy over the phone line. "Rosario, sorry, it's UPS and they need me to sign, so I have to go, but—oh, look! Deanne just got up." Her desperate look begged Deanne to play along with the ruse. "Hold on. I'll let you talk to her."

Rosario clucked. "Oh, dear. I hope the phone didn't wake her after you took such pains to let her rest."

"N-no. It's okay. She looks"—*unbelievably gorgeous*—"well-rested." She covered the mouthpiece with her thumb and tugged Deanne into the entryway with her free hand.

"Hurry up," she rasped. "It's your mom. She thinks—"

"You told her—?" Deanne paled.

"No, I said you were still sleeping." She raised a finger and gave what she hoped was a stern look. "But I don't like being cornered like this, Dee. Not one bit—"

"I'll talk to her, I promise. I just didn't know how to tell her without breaking her heart." Expression wounded, Deanne held out a hand and snapped her fingers toward her palm. Paloma relinquished the phone, fighting to dam up the flood of guilt Deanne's words had released.

As Deanne stood in the foyer talking to her mother as if nothing were wrong, Paloma wobbled back to the armchair, taking a moment to remove the nefarious action figure before she sat this time. Elbows on her knees, she furrowed her fingers into the front of her hair, and rested her forehead in her palms.

Tension pounded behind her temples. This was more difficult than she'd ever imagined.

Holy shit. She hadn't considered Rosario.

Or the rest of the family, for that matter.

She'd imagined her relationship, the core of it, involved two people: her and Deanne. Wrong. They'd been together so long, their lives and families were tightly woven, bound together in an intricate chain of love and time and promises. This would be painstaking, unraveling their lives without snapping all the threads in the process.

Her chin quivered.

God...she didn't want to lose Rosario.

She thought of Pep and Teddy's round, cinnamon-scented Grandma V, and a painful lump rose in her throat. None of this was fair to the family. But should she sacrifice her own happiness just to keep the rest of her fragile world intact? Mom wouldn't hesitate to say yes, but Paloma disagreed. She'd done that enough already, and look where it had gotten her.

She listened to Deanne stammer about the football party, selfishly grateful *she* was on the spot instead of Paloma. Damnit, they needed to talk, make some plans so they wouldn't run into this again. This was about more than a few packed suitcases and painful, moonlit good-byes. Why were they dragging their feet? Couples separated every day. *Other couples. Not us.*

"Okay, Mama," Paloma heard Deanne say, and she glanced up.

Mistake.

Dee looked freshly showered, the short, tousled black hair at her nape still damp. Well-faded jeans hugged her runner's thighs and ass, emphasizing taut strength and sleek musculature. The off-white chambray shirt molded the sculptural beauty of Dee's back, and the whole picture of this woman she knew so well stole Paloma's breath. She knew the feel of those muscles from memory, the smell of her skin, the taste of her.

God, she loved Deanne's body. Loved *her*. Paloma's mouth

went dry from the unfulfilled yearning, and the yoga tank and fitted pants she'd donned felt suddenly too revealing. These days they'd spent apart, the prospect of never being intimate with Deanne Vargas again had jacked Paloma's sex drive into the triple-X range. She'd always found Deanne's particular brand of femininity impossible to resist.

Damn her for a traitor, she wanted Dee. Wanted to make love with her until their troubles faded to moans and shudders, then curl into her chest and sleep against that steady, familiar heartbeat. The signals Paloma's body were emitting throbbed loud and clear.

As if she were throwing fists full of pheromones, Deanne spun toward her and their eyes locked. Dee's expression transformed from confusion to sexual awareness with a subtle darkening. She'd always been able to read desire on Paloma's face…and elsewhere.

Paloma crossed her arms over her chest indignantly. Painfully hard nipples didn't mean anything. She could be cold, for God's sake. *But I'm not.* That telltale heat crawled up her flesh to her throat, and she still couldn't tear her eyes away from Deanne.

"I love you, too," Dee said into the receiver, as though sensing Paloma's thoughts. Her gaze never leaving Paloma's face.

Enough! Paloma jerked her attention away and rubbed the goose bumps on her arms, at odds with this bold rush of mixed emotions. Desire. Annoyance. Need. Ache.

"I'll get back to you. Promise." A pause, and then in a lower, huskier tone. "I'll tell her. Bye."

Deanne clicked off the phone and set it on the hall table. Thumbs tucked in the pockets of her jeans, she hung her head. An uncomfortable silence threatened to swallow them both. Paloma cleared her throat, and Dee looked up.

"T-tell me what?" Paloma's voice sounded squawky to her own ears. She watched Dee's throat move.

"Mom wanted me to be sure to tell you how much I love and appreciate you." It sounded like an accusation.

"I didn't say anything to her about…this."

"I know." With a sigh, Dee moved into the living room and sank onto the couch. Legs spread wide, she interlaced her fingers behind her head, leaned back, and stared at the ceiling. Pent-up tension showed in the rhythmic bouncing of her heels. "God. I hate this, P."

Paloma straightened the armrest covers with jerky motions. "Why haven't you told her yet? What if one of the boys had said something? I thought I was gonna die."

Dee's head rolled to the side, pinning her with a level stare. "Yeah? Well, I feel like I'm going to die a lot these days, so join the club." Another tense silence yawned. When Deanne spoke again, her tone was lower. "I haven't told her because I hardly believe it myself. I don't want it to be true." There was no vehemence in her tone, just…defeat. Dee closed her eyes. "I'm sorry if you can't understand that."

"I can." Sourness assailed Paloma's middle, and she wound her hands into a fist and squeezed. "I didn't mean to fly off. She just caught me by surprise."

"You and me both."

"We should talk about things, Deanne. The boys. The truth. And our families, which sucks, but it has to be faced. There's a lot to be worked out." She stood, smoothing the front of her already smooth yoga pants. "Can I get you anything? Have you eaten?"

"You don't have to wait on me, Paloma. I never expected that."

Paloma's posture straightened. "I'll make coffee."

Deanne glanced from her wife to the long, tubular gym bag on the chair with her water bottle and keys. "Look, if I caught you on your way out—"

"No, this is more important and you're already here, so…" Paloma shrugged, then continued through the archway that led to the kitchen and breakfast nook. She spoke over her shoulder.

"I'm too late for yoga anyway. The boys were absolute demons this morning and I've been two steps behind ever since."

Ugh. Small talk. She couldn't bear it. She stood at the sink and filled the coffee carafe with cold water, staring without really seeing out into the backyard. How strange to be merely *civil* to a woman she'd loved since childhood. The sooner they could get past all this "legal" business and move on, the better. When she turned, Deanne stood in the archway, studying her with those inscrutable deep brown eyes.

"You're taking yoga?" Deanne's gaze traced the scooped neckline of her skimpy royal blue tank.

Paloma ignored the suggestive trail of her gaze and suddenly noted the cut on Deanne's chin, held together with a butterfly bandage and framed with an aura of bruising. Why hadn't she seen it before? Standing on tiptoe—damn tall counters—she poured the water into the coffee machine. "What happened to your chin?"

Shoulder braced against the wall, Deanne crossed her arms. "I had a car accident. When did you start taking yoga?"

The carafe hit the countertop with a glass-on-granite clank. "An accident? When? Please tell me it wasn't in the Chevelle?" That restored muscle car was Deanne's pride and joy.

"No." She raised the pads of her fingers gingerly to the chin injury. "At work. Tell me about yoga."

She waved the persistent and irrelevant questions away, jangling the carafe into its spot on the warmer. "It's just a damn class, Deanne. Something to fill my days."

So.

There it was.

Deanne had crashed her cruiser at work and no one thought to call? She was still Deanne's wife, the other mother of their sons, and she deserved—wait. She was acting like a territorial idiot. Nervous fingers lit on her temples before raking through her hair.

Stop it.

But she couldn't. Jealousy's ugly, unnamed cousin took up residence below her breastbone, making her want to lash out. She took her time measuring coffee grounds into the filter and starting the brew cycle. When she felt able to speak calmly, she turned. Her gaze settled on the angry wound, and she couldn't keep her voice from trembling. "Why didn't you tell me, Deanne?"

"Why didn't you tell me about yoga class?"

Her voice sharpened. "When was the last time you gave a single thought to how I spent my days or nights?"

Pain flashed over Deanne's face. "That's completely unfair, Paloma—"

"No, wait. Wait. You're right." She spun toward the sink and gripped the edge until her knuckled whitened, breathing deeply to regain her composure. "I don't want to fight. Honestly. We never fight—"

"No, we don't. Maybe…that's not so good."

She heard the rustle of Deanne's jeans behind her. Swallowed. "You want to fight?"

"No. But maybe if you had vented when things got to be too much for you, it wouldn't have come to this."

Was it true?

Should she have hollered when she felt like it?

Told Deanne when small irritants nagged at her until they became big issues?

She'd been so well trained to smile sweetly and keep petty grievances and dirty laundry to herself, but her doubts about her mother's favorite lesson were mounting. Fuck, she was practically straight, if she thought about it. The good little wife. She and Deanne were better than this.

"I don't know. It's just…" Paloma turned and shrugged helplessly. Her tone softened. "You had a car accident, and I didn't even know. I've known everything about you for the past seventeen years, Dee. It's just weird."

Deanne spread her arms and looked around. "I don't live

here anymore, remember? I didn't think you'd care that I had a little fender bender at work."

"Of course I care."

A tortured sound pushed out from deep within Deanne. "I consider myself pretty well-versed in being a woman who loves women, but this time? I don't understand what you want from me. Details about my life or for me to get out of yours?"

God, Paloma didn't want Deanne out of her life. She wanted her back in their life...but like it used to be. And, that was impossible. Couldn't Dee see that?

She approached Deanne and reached tentative fingers up to touch the bandage, careful to keep her voice neutral. "I care." She sniffed. "And I'm glad it was a patrol car and not the Chevelle. Stitches?"

"No." Deanne's tone was husky. Arms tensed at her sides, she stood very still, watching Paloma beneath those crazy-thick lashes. Her breaths came slowly, measured.

Paloma traced the small bandage again, aware of the runaway pulse in Deanne's muscular neck, the aching softness of Dee's skin on her fingertips. Some wild, idiotic part of her wanted to rise up on her toes and kiss Deanne there, and on her throat, her chest, just to see if she could incite any kind of reaction. A weak voice inside urged Paloma to invite Deanne to bed for the day, just like she used to. So difficult to be near Deanne and not want...

Don't do it, Paloma. It will only complicate things.

Her gaze flittered up to Dee's eyes, and she read confusion, pain, and scarcely banked desire, too. She was sending mixed messages. Unfair. Clenching her jaw, she curled her fingers into her palm and pulled her hand back until it lay clutched against her chest. "I'm sorry."

"Don't be. I'm not." Deanne wrapped one of Paloma's auburn curls around her finger, rubbing the strands with her thumb.

Easing away, Paloma moved stiffly to the far end of the breakfast nook and took a seat, avoiding eye contact. Coffee gurgled, the only sound in the otherwise silent house. Its rich scent spiced the charged air, but when Paloma reached up to scratch her face, the scent of Deanne's soap on her fingers was all she could smell. What was happening to her? "I'm thinking about college," she blurted, eager to obliterate the painful awareness crackling between them.

It took Deanne a moment to reply, but thankfully, she followed Paloma's lead. "That's wonderful. You should go."

"Yeah?" Paloma felt suddenly vulnerable, knocked off axis. "It makes me nervous. I'll be older than everyone."

The corners of Deanne's mouth tipped down in sync with that familiar "not a problem" shrug. "You have life experience, baby. Don't devalue that." She chewed on the inside of her cheek for a moment, still standing in the archway. "You could have taken yoga or gone to college any time, P. You know that, right? I would have supported any dream you had. I *do* support any dream you have."

Paloma bit her lip for a moment. "I guess I wasn't ready until now." And perhaps that had been a mistake. If she'd had more of a stake in her own life, she might've held Dee's attention.

"Did I hold you back?" Deanne asked, tone morose, regretful, laced with pain.

Paloma considered it. "No."

"Because if I did—"

"You didn't, honey. I would tell you."

Deanne expelled a caged breath. "God, I love you, Paloma. I love you so much, I don't know where to put it, don't know how to deal."

Chest tight, Paloma met her wife's eyes across the room.

Deanne shoved off the wall and stepped cautiously closer, as though trying to gauge Paloma's reaction. "I love you," she repeated, more passionately, "I'm in love with you, and none of that will ever change. Whatever I did, I'm sor—"

"Dee…please don't."

"No." Deanne tossed her plea aside with an impatient

motion. "I have to say it. If it really is over, I at least want you to know the truth."

Paloma glanced over the countertop that separated the nook from the kitchen, chewing the insides of her cheeks to buy time before answering. "I love you, too. But I can't live like this anymore, don't you see? *Damnit!*" Her voice cracked, and she bit down good and hard to control the painful ache in her throat.

"Okay." Deanne's calm but intense voice soothed her. "I hear you, baby girl, loud and clear." Dee continued to advance on her, then squatted and captured one of Paloma's hands between her own, massaging the knuckles as her words caressed Paloma's soul. "I may not have heard you before, but I do now. You have my undivided attention. If we love each other, we can find a way out of this together. God knows, I…I want you to be happy. It's all I've ever wanted."

It all sounded good. Yeah. But if Paloma gave in, that would mean settling. Again. After a brief honeymoon phase, Deanne would fall back into her workaholic pattern, things would once again turn lonely, and then Paloma would be stuck. She shored up her resolve. "If you want me to be happy…then you have to go."

The caresses stopped. Deanne looked away. After a long pause, Deanne's ravaged gaze swung back to meet hers. Paloma saw moisture there, which shocked her. Like her, Deanne hardly ever cried. Such paragons of control. Ha.

"Me leaving would make you happy?"

The pause stretched. Paloma shrugged one shoulder, desperation swelling inside her. "I don't…it's all I know to do at this point."

Deanne's lips pressed into a hard line, then she pushed to her feet and claimed the chair across from Paloma. She settled her elbows on Teddy's Batman placemat, looking life weary, so goddamn bleak. "Tell me what you want from me, then."

Paloma's words came in a jumbled rush. "I don't want us to be enemies, Deanne. I'm tired of being angry. What's done is done. For the boys' sake—"

"Punky." Deanne splayed her hands across her chest. "Haven't you heard a word I've said? I could never be your enemy. I. Love. You. You're the love of my life."

Paloma smiled sadly. So easy to say now. What about the past several years, when Deanne had gotten so wrapped up in work that she'd rarely even smiled? Burning questions roiled in Paloma's chest. What'd she have to lose? "Why haven't you touched me? Why haven't we made love in so long?"

Deanne's brows dipped, and she blinked in confusion. "B-because you had no interest, obviously."

Oh, now it was her fault. "You're so sure?"

Deanne spread her arms wide. "I may not be Ms. Intuition, but there are things I do understand. Your signals have always been pretty damn clear."

"Maybe you were misreading them. Maybe it hurt that you didn't want to make love." She leaned closer across the small table. "Did you ask or try?"

"Did you?" Deanne reached over and grabbed Paloma's upper arm gently. "Why couldn't you just tell me what you needed? When was the last time *you* came on to me? You used to do it all the time. When you wanted me, you took me." Dee let her eyes wander down Paloma's body. "When was the last time you showed me anything but cold, polite, scary distance? I'm not a mind reader."

Emie's identical words rushed into her mind, and guilt cracked down like a judge's gavel on Paloma's brain. Exasperated and unsure, she sighed, tangling her fingers in her hair. "It's not just…the sex. That's not what this is about. I shouldn't have brought that up. Forget it."

"I don't want to forget it." Deanne's thumbs moved in slow, intoxicating circles on her arm. "If it's lovemaking you want, baby girl, then we're on the same page. Believe me. Say the word and I'll take you upstairs right now and show you how much I love you, how much I want—"

"Stop." Paloma wrenched away, jerking her palms toward Deanne stiffly. "Just stop. It's moved beyond that. I don't want you to make love to me to prove a fucking point."

A sound of feminine indignation pushed up from inside Deanne, and Paloma knew she wasn't going to let the disturbing seductive talk drop. God, she wished Deanne would.

"It wouldn't be to prove anything. It would—"

"Deanne, pleas—"

"—be two people who love each other, who want—"

"No more. Seriously." Paloma interjected, unable to hear another word about lovemaking. It hurt too much. Making love wouldn't cure their problems, and she couldn't bear the painful throbbing the topic conjured.

She sighed, pressing two fingers to the sharp pain in her forehead. Her eyes drifted closed. "What I want is to figure out how we're going to tell our families. How we'll handle time with the boys. That's what we should be discussing. Not making love, please—"

"Fine, I got it," Deanne said, sharply.

Paloma's face lifted. Deanne's expression told Paloma she'd immediately regretted the harshness of the statement.

Gritting her teeth, Deanne took a moment to still the taut air between them, the muscle in her temple jumping. "Okay," she said, softer. "I'm sorry. But hear me when I say I don't want this. I want our life back. And I *want* you," she added pointedly. "I've wanted you since sophomore English class. Believe it."

Paloma stood and moved past Dee into the kitchen, preparing their coffee with wooden motions. Dee's eyes burned into her, but she concentrated on her task, on slowing her pounding heart. On ignoring what Deanne insisted on telling her.

I want you.

She carried the mugs back to the table and set one in front of Deanne with a decisive clunk, determined to stay on track. "What are we going to do about the get-together at your mom's?" Did

Deanne truly want to make love to her right now? Desire swirled hot and low and wet within her. "You could tell her you have to work. She'd believe that."

Deanne's wistful gaze had settled on the family photos above the buffet, and Paloma tracked it. The boys as babies, school pictures, a family photo…and her favorite candid wedding shot, laughing just after she'd committed the most heinous of errors and shoved cake in Deanne's face.

"She'd still want you and the boys there."

"True." Paloma made a mental note to put the wedding picture away.

"Besides, she knows I'm on vacation." Deanne scrubbed a palm over her face.

An unfamiliar bitterness flared inside Paloma, and she turned her attention from the photo wall. "You never take vacation."

Deanne sipped her coffee. "Well, after the crash, Obermeyer strongly suggested I get my head together. That or visit the department shrink, probably." Her lips twisted ruefully. "Eh, what the hell? It's been too long since I've taken time off anyway."

No goddamn kidding. Paloma wanted to ask why they hadn't enjoyed more family vacations. Why they hadn't stolen a weekend now and then to rekindle the flames that used to burn so hotly between them. She didn't, but the kick of resentment wouldn't disappear. "How long will you be off?"

"Open-ended. I guess that depends…"

Surely it didn't depend on her. Deanne Vargas didn't let garden-variety emotions like heartbreak interfere with her tunnel-vision work ethic. "So, what about the football party?"

Dee quirked one eyebrow. "We could just go. The boys would love it. What could it hurt?"

"Deanne." Paloma's tone was droll but tender. "We can't lie. We have to tell her. All of them. It's not fair to the boys."

A little ray of hope fizzled in Deanne's eyes, turning them dull and flat. "Fine, P, I'll tell them. I'll tell everyone that we're just another sad family statistic. Another argument against gay marriage. Because we're no better than anyone else, and we just can't make it work."

Paloma lifted her chin, refusing to let Deanne goad her into an argument. "Do that. The sooner the better."

Deanne drank, watching her over the cup's rim. "What's the next step in your grand plan to reach the greener grass on the other side?"

Paloma's spine bristled, but she forged ahead. "Some kind of legal mediation."

"We're not legally married, remember?"

Her hands tightened around her mug. "I know. But we need to put the boys first."

"Jesus, Paloma." Deanne shot to her feet, stalked to the doorway, then spun back. "You've got this whole thing scheduled and booked, don't you? How long have you been planning to leave me?"

"Deanne—"

"An opportunity to make things better"—she held up a finger, sarcasm lacing her words—"a single second chance to save two decades of love would've been downright considerate of you."

Paloma shot to her feet. "I'm trying to make things easier, not harder."

Deanne braced one hand high on the jamb. A muscle in her biceps ticked. "We haven't been apart a month yet, and you're talking what amounts to a divorce. What's easy about that?"

Paloma crossed the room, softened her tone. "Why prolong the agony?"

Deanne's disbelieving expression caved into resignation. "Fine. Mediation. But, for the record, separating children from a mother who loves them just as much as you do *isn't* in their best interest." She knocked the side of her fist on the wall twice before turning to leave.

Paloma's breathing constricted. She didn't want Deanne to walk away with bad feelings. "Dee—!"

Deanne whirled back. "Oh, yeah. One last thing." In a

single, powerful stride, she stood right before Paloma, her chest at Paloma's eye level.

Paloma peered up. Deanne's nostrils flared, and she paused only briefly before reaching around to smooth one hand against the small of Paloma's back and drive the other one into the side of her hair. She pulled Paloma against her body. Deanne's gaze touched her lips first, but her mouth was quick to follow.

The kiss attacked like a Rocky Mountain zephyr wind, unexpected and all-encompassing, leaving Paloma disoriented and breathless and wanting. Dee's tongue controlled her mouth, caressing, tasting, probing. She molded Paloma's curves against her much firmer runner's body, the not-so-subtle thrust of her hips a striking reminder of their earlier discussion.

Paloma's limbs went heavy and numb, and her body readied for Deanne in a flash of heat and moisture. Starved for Deanne's touch, Paloma didn't even think of pulling away until Dee already had. As Dee released her, Paloma stumbled forward, stunned to see Deanne widening the distance between them as if nothing had happened.

"W-what are you doing?" The words were a gasp.

"Leaving. Because that's what will make you happy, and I *am* listening. Though you may not believe it, everything I have ever done, wrong or right, baby girl, was to make you happy."

Deanne turned toward her. The back of her hand went gently to her mouth, but her eyes never left Paloma's face. When she spoke, her voice was shaky with sexual desire. "I wanted to make love to you, P, all those months. I ached with it. Still do." As if to emphasize the point, she glanced down at her own hardened nipples, then back at Paloma. "I'm only sorry I didn't do it when I still had the chance."

Deanne didn't let her respond, and Paloma jumped when the door slammed, squeezing her eyes shut. She sank to the floor and tucked her knees to her chest. Her skin hummed and her brain buzzed. She wanted to hurt, but couldn't feel a thing.

She had never been more confused in her life.

CHAPTER FOUR

Voicemail message from Paloma for Deanne, left on her brother Ruben's answering machine, Friday, September 14

Hi, Deanne, and, uh, Ruben. It's Paloma. Anyway, Dee I made an appointment with the mediator. Monday morning, ten o'clock. Unless I hear otherwise, I expect you'll be there. Just, um, meet me in the office. The address is on that paperwork I sent. Thanks. Bye.

❖

An unsent letter from Deanne to Paloma, dated Saturday, September 15

Dear Punky:

You've been avoiding me for almost a week now, ever since we kissed. I understand you want space. I'm trying to respect that, but it's not easy.

I got your message about mediation, but I want you to know something. I agreed to go only because you're holding all the cards. I'm afraid if I say no, you'll serve me with some sort of papers that will keep me from the boys, so fast my head will spin. I don't want to go, P. Mediation sessions, lawyers—anything that brings me

*closer to losing you forever is a bad idea in my book.
I'm not ready to give up on us. I'll never be ready.*

*Look, things went sour. Okay? I see now how wrong
I was to think that ignoring the tension would make it
go away. And, yes, I sensed it, but, I didn't know what
to do. You never gave me a warning. I can apologize
until my throat's sore and make promises you'll never
believe, but where will that get me?*

*I'm going to find a way to make things right
between us. Somehow. I'll win you back if it kills me, I
just have to find a way. We belong together, baby girl. I
cannot bear the thought of life without you. I love you.
So much.*

*God, who am I kidding? I can't send this. You'd
just fight me harder if you read it.*

Damn, Punky...

I always did love your fire.

Deanne pulled into Ruben's cracked driveway at eight thirty on Monday morning, looking, feeling, and probably smelling like roadkill. She'd spent a tumultuous weekend wasting tanks of gas and sleeping in her car when the exhaustion took over, feeling so desperate and heartsick, she couldn't face Ruben or anyone.

It began as aimless driving, sucking up pavement and waiting for the pain to subside. But around dusk on Saturday, it occurred to Deanne that she'd systematically visited all the old haunts that jogged happy memories about Paloma.

She traced the route she used to walk Paloma home from school. Parked by the weeping willow in old Harold Fitzmiller's yard—the site of her and Paloma's first kiss. It had tasted like bubblegum lip gloss and felt like heaven, and even though Paloma had giggled during the most serious moment in Deanne's life to that point, she'd never recovered. Paloma had ensnared her with a velvety laugh and one sweet kiss.

Dee lunched at the pizza joint where they'd go after football games, remembering those stolen back-booth kisses that made her teammates cup hands around their mouths and holler, "Get a room, Vargas!" Paloma'd always hated that.

As darkness fell, Deanne drove to the secluded parking spot overlooking the Denver skyline where they'd first made love. In a fucking car. Such a cliché, but damn, what a memory. They were just kids then, the summer before their senior year. Too young to be making love, but too blinded by emotion to refrain. The pope himself couldn't have kept them apart that sultry July night. The moon had been their candlelight, the crickets their music. Afterward, Deanne knew her life's goal was to claim Paloma as her partner and make love to her until the day she died.

Parked in their spot, Deanne had reclined her seat and allowed memories of Paloma smiling up through her tears that night flood her veins. She felt Paloma's shaky fingers tracing her lips, heard her tremulous voice whispering, "I love you, Deanne Vargas. Forever and a day."

And then, Deanne wept for all the magic she so desperately didn't want to lose. Paloma might not have a tear to shed over their love, but Deanne had a river of them.

Her grief finally spent, she wrote her the letter, then realized she couldn't send it. So she'd slept until Sunday morning, then filled the day with more of the same. Now, after five hundred miles of wear and tear on the Chevelle's tires and two nights sleeping cramped behind the wheel, Deanne resigned herself to the damnable mediation meeting. She couldn't see another maneuver around the obstacle. Even the wildest horse could only buck so long before breaking.

Deanne wrenched out of the Chevelle, groaning as she straightened. She let herself into the kitchen door off the side of the house. Ruben, her oldest brother at thirty-nine and the only divorced one out of the five, sat hunkered over the table eating Cocoa Krispies and scanning the newspaper. Some bobbed blonde chattered in the background, a boxed American smile to keep lonely people company in the morning.

Ruben peered up. His thick brows dipped. "The hell you been, Dee?"

"Nowhere." Deanne rustled up a mug and filled it with her brother's lethal brew. "Driving. Trying not to lose my mind." Glancing over her shoulder, Deanne noticed her brother wasn't wearing his usual construction site attire of jeans, a T-shirt, and steel-toed boots. As the owner of a small but growing concrete contracting company, he usually worked six on, one off. So, why the sweats and slippers on a Monday?

Deanne gave a jerk of her chin. "What's the deal—you off today?"

"Yeah. Waiting on permits, but those jokers from the county are sitting on their hands. I won't mention where their thumbs are." He shook his head. "No sense paying the guys to play Old Maid for eight hours." A pause. An assessment. "What about you? Haven't seen you in the blues for a while."

"Off until further notice." Deanne sipped, grimaced. "Sergeant doesn't want me back until I get my life worked out."

Ruben snorted. "That'll be the day."

One corner of Deanne's mouth lifted. Her brother had been really patient with this extended, brooding silence. She owed him an explanation. "You mind sticking around while I shower?" Deanne walked toward the basement stairs. "I need to talk."

"No prob. I'll be here and all ears." Ruben indicated the answering machine with a disinterested flick of his spoon. "You have some messages."

"Okay." Deanne took another tentative sip of the black, bitter coffee her brother revered, and grimaced. "Shower first, messages later. I can't stand myself a moment longer."

"I second that emotion, sis."

Half an hour later, Deanne emerged from the basement feeling like a new woman—at least hygienically speaking. In deference to the mediation meeting, she wore brown slacks and a green, navy, and brown plaid shirt Paloma had bought her last

Christmas. As promised, Ruben still sat at the table, engrossed in the crossword puzzle. He looked up, the edge of the paper rustling in his hand.

"What's a five-letter word for *postulate*?"

"Hell if I know." Deanne pointed at her mug. "You mind if I make a fresh pot? This motor oil is apt to kill us both."

"Go for it. Wuss. But if it looks like herbal tea or tastes like French vanilla, you're dead. Fair warning."

Deanne smirked, then crossed to the cupboard, hunting for the filters and grounds.

Ruben tapped the tip of his pencil on the paper. "You had another call, too."

Dee looked from the machine to her brother, hope blowing through her like bubbles. "Paloma?"

"Nope."

Ah, well. Then she didn't care. She set her jaw and turned to the coffeemaking task with a new heaviness in her chest. What did she think? That Paloma would suddenly have a change of heart and beg her to come back? About as likely as Dee coming up with a five-letter word for *postulate* off the top of her head.

After setting the pot to brew, Deanne walked to the table and pulled out a chair with her foot. She sank into it, raking fingers through her hair, then regarded Ruben over the annoyingly cheery cereal box. Of all her brothers, Ruben might understand Dee's plight. His wife, Merrilee, had left him two years earlier because he "didn't communicate." Whatever happened to the appeal of the strong silent type?

Ruben had persevered through the pain, but Deanne had noticed her stoic brother had been even quieter since Merrilee had shattered his world. The Vargas siblings were all too tenderhearted for their own damn good.

His eyes focused on the puzzle spread out before him, Ruben sniffed. "I'm listening, Deanne."

"She kicked me out."

Ruben's crossword concentration didn't waver, but he nodded sagely. "Not a news flash, genius, since you've been camped on the hide-a-bed from hell for two weeks. Didn't entertain any illusions that I'd suddenly become more fun than Li'l Bit." A pause. "Does Mom know?"

"Not yet."

Ruben's brows flicked up and back down. "You hope."

"What do you mean?"

Her brother hiked one meaty shoulder. "Mom's pretty sharp. Can't pull too much over on her. I would've thought you learned that back in high school. She knew you and Paloma were together before *you* knew you were together." He thrust his chin forward, scratching the fleshy underside with nonchalance.

Deanne blew out a tired breath. "I can't make myself believe it's true, Rube. I keep thinking Paloma will come to her senses. Mom was so angry with Merrilee. I don't want that to happen with P. They get along so well."

Ruben blinked at her. "Which is why you oughtta tell her before she hears it from my nephews or tricks me into spilling it. That'd hurt her, you and Li'l Bit keeping such a big thing from her like that." His eyes dropped to the puzzle. "Just a suggestion. I'm no expert. You gotta do what feels right."

"Going home would feel right." Deanne paced to the coffeemaker and filled her mug. Turning back, she leaned against the counter and braced her hands on the edge, spread wide. She crossed one ankle over the other. "I don't want to lose my family. Telling Mom makes it…more real."

The chair legs squeaked beneath Ruben's stocky form as he leaned back. "Take it from me, kiddo, denial won't make it go away."

Deanne knew he was right. "Want to know the worst part? I've known something was bothering Paloma for months, maybe longer." She tried to smile through her chagrin, but only one half of her mouth cooperated. "Thought if I ignored it, things would improve."

Ruben's eyes looked baleful in his round face. "I hear you, Dee. Like a freaking echo."

"Yeah." All Deanne's brothers lived nearby, but she hadn't thought twice before coming to Ruben's. She wrapped cold fingers around the warm mug and returned to her seat. "What should I do?"

"My honest opinion?" Ruben leaned in, his tone adamant.

"Brutally."

"Fight for her, Deanne. Whatever it takes, whatever you sacrifice, go the distance." He pointed one thick finger. "Don't give up or back down, or you'll regret it for the rest of your life." Ruben's chubby face fell.

Deanne ached for him, for his loss of Merrilee. "You miss her, Rube?"

"Constantly. If I had just one more chance to get her back, I'd blabber on till I lost my voice. But I don't." He paused. "You still have a chance with Paloma. Don't let it slip away."

Deanne shook her head slowly. "How'd we wind up like this?"

Ruben pursed his lips, thinking. "You're the youngest. I'm the oldest. For whatever reason, I think we took what happened between Mom and Victor more to heart than Tony, Frank, and Randy did, and it shaped us in certain ways."

"And that's bad?" Deanne shrugged. "I thought I'd learned from Victor's mistakes so I wouldn't repeat them."

Ruben lumbered up from his chair and got a cup of coffee. "We didn't repeat his, sis. We made our own. Hell, I hold everything inside. You're a workaholic—"

"You think I'm a workaholic?" Deanne frowned.

Ruben's droll glance had "duh" written all over it.

Deanne traced her finger over a scratch in the oak tabletop and considered this. "Huh. I never thought of myself that way. After how Victor left Mom, I never wanted that kind of heartache to touch my family. So I work hard, yeah, but only because I know it's what he *wouldn't* have done."

"Rationalize it all you want, but it doesn't change the fact you're a workaholic." Ruben hooked one foot over the other. "Victor is a big part of who we turned out to be, like it or not."

The thought sickened her. She hated to wonder if she'd driven her wife away in a blind attempt to keep her. How fucking ironic would that be? She glanced at the clock, uncomfortable with the direction the conversation had taken. "I've got to hit it. But…"

"Spit it out."

"Suppose I fight so hard that it only pushes her further away?"

Ruben held her gaze for a long time, just shaking his head. "What've you got to lose? You're at rock bottom, kiddo. Claw your way up or lie there and die, your choice. I'm just experience talking, and"—he indicated the liberal gray shot through his black hair—"it ain't pretty."

The phone rang. "You get it," Ruben said, pushing off the counter. "Damn thing never rang until you started shacking here."

Deanne smiled as she stood. "You know I appreciate you listening, everything."

"I just hope some of it got through." Ruben reached over and knocked on Deanne's head. "Aside from being a workaholic, you're also pretty thick." He jerked his chin toward the phone as it rang a third time. "And I'm not your damn social secretary, little sis. Answer the phone."

Deanne watched her brother leave the room and scooped it up on ring four. "Hello?"

"Vargas? It's Nora." Her voice held notes of relief and exasperation. "Why haven't you called me back?"

"Sergeant O, I—" she glanced at the clock. She hadn't figured work would call during this imposed vacation. "I was gone all weekend. Just got in. What's up?"

"Where was your pager? Your cell? No, forget it. You're on vacation. Have you forgotten what today is?"

Today? Deanne leaned her hip against the counter. Hmmm, well, it was Monday. Possibly the first day of the end of her marriage, but Obermeyer wouldn't call for—September 17—goddamn it! Urgency jerked Deanne to attention. She back-hammered her fist against the cupboard door. "The sergeant's test. I completely forgot—"

"Well, don't stand there stammering. Get your ass in the car and blaze down to headquarters. If you don't take it today, you can't take it again until next year."

Horror washed through Deanne like cold poison. The exam. The mediation. "But—"

"You want the promotion or not? I'll meet you there with your paperwork. Leave now or you'll never make it."

Deanne couldn't reply.

"Vargas?"

War waged inside Deanne's heart and mind. Granted, she didn't want to wait until next year. She'd been studying for the difficult test for months. Then again…Paloma. And the mediation appointment.

An appointment to end their marriage.

The realization struck Deanne like an uppercut, leaving her dazed with its wrongness. She was surrendering way too easily, exactly what Ruben had warned against. She didn't *want* to start the process of permanently destroying their family, be it mediation or obtaining lawyers. Dee didn't dare take even one step toward that unfathomable end.

Don't give up or back down, or you'll regret it for the rest of your life.

Her fist clenched. Ruben was right. Deanne had to fight Paloma's "why prolong the agony?" excuse. P was running scared, that's all. They had so many opportunities to work things out before it came to all the legal, formal crap, and Deanne wouldn't back down until she convinced her of that.

Resolute, she set her jaw. "I'll meet you at headquarters. Just let me grab my cell phone. I need to make a call on the way."

❖

"I'm sorry to make you drive down here. I just didn't know what to do." Truthfully, Paloma couldn't summon the energy to get in her car and drive away. Instead, she and Emie sat huddled in uncomfortable chairs in the stark waiting room of the mediation offices.

"Don't apologize." Emie adjusted in the chair and grimaced. "Even beached whales need to get out of the house now and then."

Paloma flashed a guilty glance at her very pregnant friend. "How are you feeling?"

"Better than you at this point."

Murderers on death row probably felt better than she did right now. "I can't believe Dee didn't show. After all this." She twisted her wrist, then let her hand drop in her lap.

Ever the logical one, Emie said, "Listen, don't fly off until you know the circumstances. I'm sure something just came up, sweetie."

Paloma spread her arms. "But don't you see? Something *always* 'just comes up.' Something else is always more important than me and this so-called marriage, and I'm forever forced to give in."

Emie quirked her mouth to the side. Paloma didn't envy her the position of designated sympathizer—nothing could soothe this ache.

"You want to know the worst part?" Paloma's self-derisive laugh held no humor. "Last week, she came over and...she kissed me." She flashed Emie an assessing glance, but read no judgment in her gaze. "And I mean, *really* kissed me. I've spent the last week second-guessing my decision. I had almost convinced myself that Deanne *had* seen the light, that we might be able to work out this fiasco. I was planning to talk to her after this appointment. I'm pathetic."

Emie's expression shone with encouragement. "Paloma, you still can work it out. If you two clear the air, and—"

"No." Paloma stood and hiked her briefcase up on her shoulder. "Whatever stupid romantic thoughts I had are gone. This was it. If she can't even bother to show when our marriage is on the line, forget it. I don't need Deanne Vargas, and I refuse to smile and make nice anymore." She spun and headed for the double doors before Emie recognized the crushing disappointment on her face.

Deanne hadn't reached Paloma before running out the door and headed for police headquarters. She must have left early, and she never picked up her cell phone in the car. The home voicemail engaged, and Deanne opened her mouth…but nothing emerged. Paloma would likely misconstrue whatever she said, no matter the explanation, so she'd hung up without speaking. But, as her heels struck the sidewalk leading to police headquarters, she doubted herself. She had a well-developed cop's gut after eleven years on patrol, and every instinct inside her screamed, "Danger!" But she was here now. Might as well follow through.

She dragged her wallet out of her back pocket and flashed her badge at the deputy manning the metal detectors before shouldering through the arch. That nagging feeling of doom chased her through the lobby and into the long, wood-paneled hallway, warning her she shouldn't be here. She should be with Paloma. *Too late.*

"Deanne!"

She whirled back as Sgt. Obermeyer rushed to catch up. She wore jeans and a sweatshirt, a manilla folder clutched beneath her arm.

Her eyes flashed with annoyance as she neared. "I called your name about five times. Didn't you hear me?"

Deanne peered over her shoulder to the austere lobby through which she'd plowed blindly—and apparently deafly—through. "Sorry. I guess I wasn't paying attention."

"So, that getting your head together goal is going well, I see," Obermeyer muttered. She shuffled through the folder and whipped out a form. Her eyes traced the text briefly before she held it out. Deanne hardly spared it a glance before folding it into quarters and shoving it in her back pocket.

Nora shook her head, peering up at Deanne quizzically. "Are you even ready to take this test?"

"I've studied." Deanne rubbed her knuckles along her jawline.

"Vargas, what's going on?" Nora glanced at her watch, and Deanne followed suit. Still a couple minutes before the test would start, but more than half an hour late for mediation. She toyed with the idea of finding a quiet corner and pulling out her cell phone. But what could she say to Paloma now, after the fact? *I made* another *bad choice? Forgive me,* again?

"Vargas! Damnit."

Deanne frowned and shook her head as if to clear the daze. "I'm sorry." She moved aside to let a group of plainclothes officers pass, then leaned against the wall, blowing a breath out pursed lips. "I think I really screwed up. Epic fail."

"Why? What happened?" Obermeyer crossed her arms, the folder dangling from one hand.

"Paloma scheduled a mediation appointment for us today. I'd forgotten about the test so…after you called, I couldn't reach her to tell her I couldn't make it, and now—"

"Oh, no." Nora's face fell. "But the test shouldn't take you too long. What time's the appointment?"

"It *was* at ten."

"Hold up. One sec—you blew it off?" Obermeyer's eyes grew round with dismay. "You pissed away a chance to—for a stupid promotional test?" She released a short, incredulous laugh. "Did you hear nothing I told you in the office that night?"

"I heard. I listened. But my brother—" Damn, wrong choice.

Ruben had said fight *for* her, not fight *with* her. Deanne spread her arms and shrugged, a feeling of utter ineptitude blasting her like pepper spray to the face. "What now?"

"You have to ask? I should knock you upside the head." Nora grabbed a fistful of Deanne's sleeve and propelled her toward the exit without letting go. "Go to your wife, Deanne. Go! The job, promotions—none of it matters more than family—"

"I know that, but—"

"No buts," Nora snapped. "Ever. *Never* make the mistake of putting the job first."

Jesus, Nora was right. Deanne had thought she was putting her family first *by* putting the job first, but she was wrong. She picked up speed as they reached the metal detectors. They passed through one after the other, leaving the building at a jog. Nora followed her as far as the threshold before stopping. "Good luck!" she called through cupped hands. "You annoying, hardheaded woman!"

Damned hindsight and its twenty-twenty vision. The very concept irritated the shit out of Deanne. The entire drive from police headquarters to Paloma's house—their house—Deanne mentally kicked herself. Based on everything Paloma had revealed since the split, all the things that had made her unhappy, how could Deanne have thought for a moment that skipping the mediation appointment would be a wise strategic move? She banged her fist against the steering wheel. "Fuck!"

By the time she pulled in behind Paloma's car, desperation had taken hold of Deanne's brainwaves, and she didn't even think she'd be able to explain the convoluted thought processes that had led her to make such a colossally wrong decision. But she had to try.

Blood hammering through her veins, she straightened her shirt, then strode with more confidence than she felt toward the door. Emie's car, she noted, sat next to Paloma's, the engine still ticking. That could be bad. Deanne rang the bell twice, then stood back and prayed. Her throat closed when the deadbolt slid home, but it was Emie's face, not Paloma's, that peered out. Relief showed in Emie's eyes, then she eased out, closing the door behind her. "Well,it's about freaking time."

"She's here, right?"

"Oh, yeah. I don't think she'll talk to you, though. God, what happened, Deanne?"

"Damnit." She clenched everything, then released it. "It was…a work issue, but it doesn't matter. I should've blown it off and been there for Paloma."

Emie crossed her arms atop her distended belly. Her tone gently chastised, but her eyes looked almost sympathetic. "Maybe not blown it off, but you should've tried to make other arrangements, or at least said something to Paloma."

But, but, but! Deanne's mind defended, though logic said her argument sucked. "I called, but…when voicemail picked up, I didn't have the words. Damnit." She smoothed her palm down her face. "My excuses sound lame even to me, Emie. I don't want to waste your time or insult your intelligence by rattling them off. I was an ass."

A wan smile lifted one side of Emie's mouth, and her tone went wry. "Well, at least you and Pea agree on something. She's talking about serving custody papers, speaking to you only through lawyers. It's knee-jerk, honey. I'm trying to calm her and get her to a less reactive place, but—" She shrugged.

Through Deanne's haze of worry, she replayed Emie's words and did a double take. "You aren't pro-split?"

Emie socked Dee in the shoulder, but softened it with a wink. "Don't be a *complete* bonehead, Deanne. Who else but Pea would put up with an annoying workaholic like you?"

One half of Deanne's mouth cooperated with her feeble attempt at a smile. This was good, having Emie on her side. Paloma respected her friends' input. Deanne needed them to understand how desperately contrite she felt about the appointment, but the only words that came to mind were, "I don't want anyone but her. Ever."

"I know, dummy." Emie tilted her head to the side. "But I'll be honest. It doesn't look good."

Deanne cupped her elbows and hunkered down until their eyes were level. "Em, I beg you. Convince her to let me explain. I just want to tell her what was going on in my brain when I made the decision to go to work instead of meeting her. I screwed up. I get it. I don't expect forgiveness—"

"Good thing."

"I'll leave her alone for a while, give her some space after this if she'll just…listen."

Emie cast Deanne a dubious look, rolled the idea around in one cheek. "I'll try. No promises. You know how stubborn she can be."

"She's perfect," Deanne said.

Emie sighed. "Give me a sec." She tossed Deanne a playfully stern glare. "And don't make any other idiotic decisions while you wait, okay?"

Deanne pointed down. "I'm frozen to this spot."

Emie disappeared into the house, and Dee leaned against the wrought iron railing that edged the small concrete stoop. Frozen was a weak description of how she felt. Numb. Dead, even. She didn't move. Hardly breathed. She merely waited, trying to clear her mind and praying Paloma would agree to see her.

After several agonizing minutes, Paloma's stony face peered around the edge of the door, and Deanne cast up a silent vote of sainthood for Emie. She couldn't imagine how Emie had convinced Paloma to listen, but she didn't care.

Anger flashed beneath the utter disappointment Deanne read in Paloma's closed expression. "What?" Her tone was pure burning ice.

Dee pushed off the railing, but words failed her even more dismally than she'd failed Paloma. How in the hell did a woman say the right thing in this situation? What *was* the right thing? Moistening her lips with a nervous flick of her tongue, she took the plunge. "I made a terrible mistake." *State the obvious. It's a start.*

Paloma's hard expression didn't change one iota.

Flipping her hands helplessly, she forged on. "Punky, I'll tell you right now, this won't sound reasonable to you. But...if you could put yourself into my mindset, just for a minute. Please." When she didn't slam the door, as Deanne had expected, she lowered her head, shifting her weight from one foot to the other, measuring her next words.

"I've been ravaged since you left the message about mediation. Shredded. But I planned on being there." She enunciated slowly. "I really did."

Paloma's lashes fluttered, but she lifted her chin.

"Then, this morning, Nora called me at Ruben's. I haven't mentioned this, but I've been studying to take the sergeant's test for six months. It was today."

"Why didn't you call me on Friday, then?" Her voice sounded croaky and accusatory. She cleared her throat. "I even gave you an out to reschedule."

"I didn't call because I'd forgotten about the test." She splayed a palm on her chest. "My only thoughts, baby, have been about you and me. I didn't remember until Nora called me, right about the time I was heading out the door to meet you."

"But you didn't come meet me." Her words were judge, jury, and executioner, and just like that Deanne was *dead woman walking.*

A thick pause ensued. "No. But I called."

"There wasn't a message."

"I"—she uttered a sound of disgust—"didn't know what to say without making you angry."

"So you said nothing." It wasn't a question. Scorn moved over Paloma's face. "That's just perfect. Anything else?"

"Yes. Remember, think like me." Deanne finger-combed her

hair with frustration. "I chose the test because I got it into my head that agreeing to mediation was as good as telling you I'm okay with the split. Which, for the record, I'm not."

Paloma didn't so much roll her eyes as let them drift heavenward and back down.

Chagrin spread through Deanne. Clearly, Paloma wasn't swayed. "I know, it's stupid. *Now* I know. But with that in my head, I drove to headquarters instead of meeting you."

Paloma's head jerked to the side in a stiff shrug. "Well, I guess I know what really matters to you, Dee. Not that it wasn't abundantly clear already." She started to close the door. "Enjoy your promo—"

"Wait." Deanne smacked her palm against the door, urgency pulling her words out faster. "Let me finish. I didn't take the test, Punky. That's what I'm telling you. I know it's too little, too late, and I missed the appointment regardless. But I'm learning. I'm trying—Jesus, baby girl, I am trying so hard. I don't care if I have to wait until next year to go for the promotion, or if I never get it. I love you. Beyond all reason, beyond everything, I love you."

Paloma blinked rapidly, then dropped her gaze. "Is that all?"

"*I love you.* That's not *all*, that's a lot." Deanne waited, but Paloma didn't look at her. It was her most-dreaded stand-off realized. Deanne on the outside of their life looking in, Paloma's closed expression saying Deanne would never be welcome inside again. She'd almost decided to admit defeat and walk away, when Paloma's soft voice stopped her.

"The thing is, Deanne, it always takes you until after the fact to remember your family. Don't you see that?"

Dee's mouth dropped open, but she couldn't dispute Paloma's point. Perception is reality. Nora had reminded her that Paloma's perspective was the only one that truly mattered this time. It wouldn't help to explain that her awkward way of showing love was working, taking care of Paloma and the boys. But couldn't Paloma at least see how desperately Dee wanted to change? To be the kind of partner she needed? She blew out a defeated breath. "I hear you, but—"

"Because—let me finish." Paloma paused. "I see us as being last on your priority list. I feel it, too, and it hurts like hell. It's only a matter of time before the boys start to sense it, and I won't let that happen." Her regretful gaze pulled to Deanne's. "It wasn't supposed to be like this, Dee. I don't want to hurt anymore."

Remorse and pain clogged Deanne's throat as she clenched and unclenched her fists, desperate to grasp what was slipping away. She reached for her wife, but Paloma shook her head, and Deanne regretfully folded her fingers back into her palm.

The raging torment must have shown on Deanne's face, because Paloma sighed. "Don't give me that look. I don't hate you, honey. I never could. But I'm not ready to forgive you for this, either. Can you understand that?"

"Yes," she whispered hoarsely. "But I'm not ready to throw in the towel on this marriage. Can *you* understand that?"

"I understand that *you're* not. You'll have to keep the faith for both of us on that account, because at this point, Deanne, I don't see anything but...the end." She sniffed.

Deanne's heart gave one painful thud.

"I'm sorry you missed the test. I know how important it must've been for you."

"Nothing is as important as you."

Paloma huffed. "Words, Deanne. Pretty, empty words. That's all you keep giving me, and it's not enough." With that, the door snicked shut on their house and in Deanne's heart.

Paloma pressed her back against the door and squeezed her eyes shut. "Damn her," she whispered.

"Don't tell me you can't see how desperately that gal loves you, Pea. She's wrecked."

Emotion twisted and squeezed inside her. "I've already told you, Em, sometimes love isn't enough."

Emie brushed back a lock of hair that had tangled to Paloma's eyelashes. "And I'm telling *you*, sometimes it is enough, if you can find it in your heart to forgive and move on." She paused, her face a mask of sympathy and understanding. "Can't you remember what made you love Deanne in the first place?"

"Ignorance? Youth?"

"No." Emie ticked qualities off on her slim fingers. "She was goal-oriented, a hard worker, dependable. Always went the extra mile. She made you feel secure, you told me—"

"So?" Emie frowned. "That was then and this is now."

"I disagree. Dee may be taking things to extremes these days, but she still goes the extra mile. She's still that same goal-oriented, dependable hard worker—"

"Yeah," Paloma interjected. "But she used to go the extra mile for me, not work. And I don't feel secure anymore. I feel forgotten. Critical difference."

Emie sighed. "Well, Dee seems willing to work on it. Desperate to, actually."

Paloma pushed off the door and scuffed into the living room. She flung her body back on the couch. "I thought you were on my side."

"I am, dumbass. Which is why I don't want to see you throw away a life you've worked so hard to build, with a woman who is truly your soul mate. No one ever promised it would be easy, this relationship stuff." Emie spread her arms wide. "Face it, once you're dating them, women are organically annoying, with us, naturally, being the exceptions to that rule."

Paloma laughed, grudgingly.

"But girlfriends, partners, wives…they have good qualities, too. You just have to ask yourself"—Emie picked up their mugs and headed toward the kitchen—"is it worth it?"

Paloma gnawed her lip and pondered this annoyingly

rhetorical question, coming up blank. Leave it to Emie to ask the profound yet unanswerable. Jamming her arms crossed, Paloma frowned. "Well?" she yelled toward the kitchen. "Is it worth it?"

Emie didn't respond.

CHAPTER FIVE

From Paloma Vargas's journal, Monday, September 24

I had planned to attend Back-to-School Night alone, but I got a voicemail from Deanne, and she said she'd meet me there. I'm not holding my breath. I'm still angry about the mediation thing, but of course, in moments when I'm not feeling totally self-centered, I hope Dee does show up for the boys' sake. Partners or not, we're still their parents. If we can't act like adults and pull it together long enough to stay involved in Pep's and Teddy's lives, well, that's just pathetic. I'm adamant that this divorce will not affect the boys.

And...okay. Maybe I want to see Deanne just a tiny bit. Call me a hypocrite, but I wonder how she's doing after our huge argument. I don't know that I'm ready to cave in, but after several long talks with the ever-wise Emie, I can grudgingly appreciate the sacrifice Deanne made skipping the sergeant's test to try and make it to our appointment. I want to have a forgiving heart. I do. But it's hard. Still, she's been so good about staying away, giving me space, I just wonder how she's truly adapting. I worry too much about her, I know.

Me <——idiot.

I'm sick to death of the animosity, which can't be good for the kids. Still, I don't want to keep being so indecisive. Back and forth, back and forth. Dee loves the boys beyond reason. Actually, she has a lot of good qualities—no denying that. It's just the other stuff.

God, what will I do when she finds another woman?

Ugh. I feel sick.

Paloma arrived early at the school and gave in to the boys' pleas for a few minutes on the deserted playground. As long as they took care to stay clean, the chance to expend their bottle-pop energy would pay off in the long run. Better here than in front of their teachers, where she prayed they'd act like well-mannered little gentlemen.

She sat on a bench and watched them run from the slide to the swings, laughing and yelling to each other. As the evening breeze lifted her hair, Paloma closed her eyes and took advantage of the solitary time to gather her wits.

It had been a long week of anger and disillusionment since she had last seen Deanne, and the thought of sitting next to her tonight absolutely frazzled her nerves. Despite it all, Dee had had a magnetic pull on Paloma's psyche since girlhood. No sense trying to tell herself it'd be gone. That charming, solemn, devoted young woman still existed somewhere deep inside the stranger Paloma hardly knew anymore. Regrets burned her throat. If only Deanne hadn't shuttered herself away in the first place. If only she had—just once—asked Paloma what was wrong. If only she'd give Paloma more than empty promises…

Paloma sensed Deanne's presence as she approached from behind, as though her very soul emitted sensory waves that Paloma's heart alone could detect. Dee had shown up. Paloma's breath caught. *Will miracles never cease?* A blue flame of hope flickered inside her, softening her bitterness even further.

Dee moved closer, and Paloma stiffened, the hair at her nape prickling. She couldn't help but remember the living room kiss that had so shaken her resolve. Her breathing came fast and shallow when the breeze caught Deanne's singularly sexy scent and surrounded Paloma with the memories it stirred.

Paloma kept her seat but hastily smoothed her low-slung pants and tugged down her cleavage-flattering blouse—an outfit she hadn't chosen knowing she'd see Deanne, necessarily. She just wanted to look nice for the meeting with the boys' teachers. But she knew it looked hot on her, especially with the five pounds she'd lost, and a small, fickle part of her hoped Deanne would notice.

All at once, the boys caught sight of Deanne. Paloma could tell from the instantaneous brightening of their faces.

"Mommy!" they chimed in unison.

Like a high-velocity bullet, Teddy flew over the loose gravel in a flat-out sprint toward his mommy. His eyes were glued to Deanne, so he couldn't possibly see the railroad tie edging around the swings, though it lay directly in his path.

Sucking a sharp breath that smelled of wind and Deanne and grilled dinner from a nearby house, Paloma lurched to her feet. She sensed the accident before it happened.

His left foot caught on the thick wood, ripping the shoe from it. Little Teddy sailed through the air and he hit the gravel chin first, his head slamming into the metal swing set frame with a sickening clang. His neck wrenched at an angle that made Paloma flinch, and his unnatural limpness and dead silence shot pain straight to her womb.

"Teddy!" she screamed, dropping her briefcase. She ran, losing one Keen clog in the process. Her peripheral vision caught Pep running from another direction; she wanted to scream "Stop!" before they had another collision, but horror strangled her silent.

Deanne appeared at her side. She grabbed Paloma's elbow and steadied her the rest of the way. They fell to their knees next to Teddy, who still hadn't moved. Paloma's heart beat as though a demon dwelled inside it, determined to punch its way out. Her entire body shook with adrenaline. He was hurt. Really hurt.

"Oh...God. Baby!" She made ineffective jerky motions with her hands. Starting to touch him, then stopping again. She didn't want to shake him, but one primal part of her needed to rattle his cage. *Cry! Scream! Anything!*

"Teddy, hon." Deanne caressed him gently, then leaned her ear to the boy's back to listen. "Damnit, T, wake up." She felt for a pulse in Teddy's tiny neck. "Fuck," Deanne bit out, casting Paloma a severe glance. "I have to start rescue breathing. I need you to help me turn him over without compromising his neck."

"H-he's not breathing?" Paloma clutched at her throat, and the world swirled to a dark pinpoint that contained only this, only them. *Not my baby.*

Deanne wrenched off her leather jacket and tossed it aside. "Listen, run for help, Paloma—"

Suddenly, Teddy stirred, and they both froze. After one blood-gurgled inhale, his wail cut through the twilight like an off-tone siren. Paloma thought she'd never heard anything so achingly wonderful in her life. She reached for Teddy with a violently trembling hand, touching him softly.

"We're here, Teddy boy." She brushed his brow.

Deanne bent closer, running through the motions of rescue first aid again.

"Mommy?"

"I'm here, little man. Lie still, okay?"

"Mamaaaaa!" Teddy's tear-streaked face struggled to lift, and he flailed for her embrace.

"No, no, honey. Listen to Mommy. Don't move!" *Madre de Dios!* So much blood. It covered the lower half of his face, filled his nose and mouth. Not only that, but a horrible purple goose egg had risen on his head.

Rigidity hit her like a lightning bolt, and she went dead still. Pep, who'd been hanging back, took one glance at his little brother's macabre state and threw himself into her arms, shaking and silent. Paloma rubbed his slight back as she peered down at her youngest son. "M-my God. Please, Deanne—"

"Head wounds always bleed like hell," Deanne assured her in a voice more relaxed than her expression let on. "Try to stay calm. For him."

But Deanne wasn't so together on the inside. Paloma could tell just looking at her ashen complexion. Her focus completely on Teddy, Deanne bent forward until her face was on the same level as her son's.

"Hey, little man." Teddy's cries nearly drowned out her words. "This'll be one to brag about at school, eh?" As Deanne talked, she placed her leather jacket over Teddy's body.

"Mommy..." Teddy gurgled. "M-my m-moooouth!"

"Your mouth looks good, big guy," Deanne lied. "What else hurts, son?"

"My n-neck."

"Yeah? It looks good, too, T." As Deanne spoke, she gently probed the skin at the back of Teddy's small neck. He flinched, and Deanne placed a hand on his back. "You lie good and still, Teodoro. Do you hear me, guy?"

"D-don't l-leave me, Mommy!"

"I'm not going anywhere, T. Lie still." Deanne glanced at Paloma. "Babe, run and—"

"Nooooo! Mama, don't goooo!" Teddy wailed.

Paloma crouched, the coppery wet smell of her little boy's blood registering horribly in her mind before numbness could block it. *Don't think about it.* She had to keep it together for Teddy. Pep still clung to her, but he wouldn't look at his little brother. "Mama's right here, sweet baby. I'm right here." She glanced beseechingly up at Deanne. *Please don't make me leave my baby.*

"Damnit! There's no time—" Deanne pressed a rough breath through her nose and fished in her pocket for car keys. "Pep."

Pep turned toward his mommy, teeth chattering with fear.

Deanne smiled encouragingly, though Paloma could see the urgency in her cocoa brown eyes. "Can you be my partner here, buddy?" Deanne asked their son.

"Y-yes." Pep swallowed audibly.

Deanne lobbed him the keys. "Run to Mommy's car—"

"Not through the parking lot, Dee." Paloma's voice was reedy and high-pitched. "He's too upset."

Deanne rubbed her free hand up and down Paloma's back in long, soothing strokes, but her gaze locked with Pep's. "I parked just on the edge of the playground, babe. He won't even have to go into the lot. We need an ambulance. It's not a choice."

"Of course, you're right." Paloma whipped a glance around the schoolyard, but found it empty other than them. Where was everyone when they needed them?

"Pep, unlock the car and get my cell phone, son. It's in the drink holder. Can you do that?"

"Okay."

"Deanne spoke in calm, well-modulated tones, trusting eyes boring directly into her son's. "You remember how to dial nine-one-one?"

"Uh-huh. And press Send, right?" Pep tugged at his collar.

"You got it, buddy. Press Send and speak nice and clear, do you hear me? Take a good deep breath."

Paloma dragged in her own lungful of fear-tinged air as she watched Pep's skinny little chest expand and contract.

"Tell them you're my son, and that your brother is badly hurt. Good and calm. My name is Officer—?"

"Deanne Vargas," Pep obediently answered.

"From district—?"

"Four."

"Good man." Deanne clapped a hand on his shoulder and squeezed. "Ask them to send an ambulance to the school, and keep them on the line. Talk to them while you're walking back, okay? So I can talk to them after you. Got all that?"

Pep seemed to absorb calmness and confidence from his

mommy's apparent faith in his abilities. He stood straighter, face flushed. "Yeah, Mommy. I can do it."

"I know you can, *m'ijo*. Now go on."

Pep hesitated, sliding a reluctant sidelong glance toward the growing pool of blood around Teddy's chin.

"Hey." Deanne whistled sharply to redirect his attention. When Pep looked at her, Deanne winked, the waning sunset glowing rosy gold off the smile lines around her eyes. Her words, however, were firm and compelling. "Your brother will be fine, Pep. I promise. But I need you to make that call."

Pep whipped a confirming glance at Paloma, and she managed a shaky smile. "Listen to Mommy, sweetheart. Go on. Watch where you're running."

A boy with an important job, Pep took off like the wind. Paloma's eyes jerked to Teddy, who'd grown way too quiet. "His h-head, Deanne. Look at the—"

"Paloma." Deanne pressed a finger across her own lips, then pointed to Teddy. "He'll be fine. But—" She shook her head.

Paloma understood. Deanne didn't want Teddy to realize how badly he was hurt, or shock might become a real problem. Instead of talking about Teddy, Paloma wiggled down onto her stomach facing him and whispered soft reassurances. He'd lost teeth, and as Paloma collected them from the bloody gravel, she silently hoped they were baby teeth—as if there weren't more serious issues to worry about.

It seemed like forever, but in reality it was mere moments before Pep returned, the phone to his ear. A young woman Paloma recognized as the school attendance secretary trotted alongside him, and she stopped to collect the spilled contents of Paloma's briefcase.

As Pep came into hearing range, Paloma heard him saying, "Mommy's right here. Hold on." He closed the distance between them in a run, holding the phone out. "They wanna talk to you, Mommy."

Deanne sat back on her haunches and took the phone from

Pep, pulling the boy against her chest as she spoke in official-sounding phrases.

Loss of consciousness.

Possible neck or head injury.

Definite shock.

Deep laceration.

Approaching sirens tore the beautiful silence of the evening, and relief rushed through Paloma. Time seemed slow motion and distorted; she thought they'd never get here.

Pep, looking stronger for having done a man's job, leaned toward his little brother. "You have a really awesome bump on your head, but you're gonna be okay, Teddy Bedwetty."

"That's not my name," Teddy murmured in a tone utterly devoid of the vehemence with which he usually defended himself against the hated nickname.

Pep seemed to notice, growing very earnest. "Till you get better, I'll do all your chores, 'kay? And, next time we're at Auntie Gia's, you can sit in the driver's seat first."

"Swear?" Teddy mumbled listlessly.

Pep drew an X over his chest, eyes round and solemn. "Hope to die, stick a needle in my eye."

"'Kay." Teddy sucked a rattling breath.

Paloma's throat closed with an emotion she recognized as pure love, and her gaze drifted to Deanne's just as she disconnected. They had such good boys, and their shared glance acknowledged that. Deanne offered her hand, and Paloma gladly took it. Nothing mattered right now but Teddy.

The ambulance arrived, throwing blue and red lights against the trees, and disgorged the paramedics in a mad rush of glare and equipment and sound. Paloma had to literally drag herself away from Teddy's side, but Deanne was right. They needed room to work. Their clipped phrases rang like dialogue from a television episode; she couldn't bear to think of it in relation to her little boy.

Get a pressure bandage on that laceration.

Watch the C-spine.

Pep remained unusually quiet, sitting cross-legged on the grass next to her feet. Deanne pulled Paloma back against her warm, solid chest, and Paloma didn't resist. On the contrary, she felt tearfully grateful for the comfort and warmth as her wife cradled her emotionally as well as physically.

Patient's immobilized.

Start an IV.

I can't get a vein. Too small.

She shuddered, and Deanne smoothed calming palms over the goose bumps on her forearms. It felt good, she acknowledged, as she watched the paramedics work on her son.

"You know them?" She asked Deanne without turning.

Deanne's murmured "Mmm-hmm" rumbled against Paloma's back. "They're a good crew. Don't worry, baby girl."

They had braced Teddy's neck and strapped him to a backboard, securing his head to it with some sort of tape. Paloma sucked in a breath and held it as they prepared to move him.

The slim paramedic in charge said, "Okay, slowly. On my count. One, two, three."

Paloma winced as they flipped him over, but relief made her sag when she saw Teddy's eyes wide open. Deanne's warm, muscled arms around her tightened, as though she could fortify Paloma's courage with her physical and emotional strength. Paloma felt Deanne's lips against her hair whispering, "Easy, babe. He's doing good," but her heart in her throat silenced any response.

By this time, the light show had drawn a crowd. Word was sent to Pep's and Teddy's teachers, and the young secretary had taken care to brush off and return Paloma's briefcase.

After they'd secured Teddy on a gurney, Paloma, Deanne, and Pep walked alongside as the paramedics steered him toward the ambulance. It became a jumble of motion and outstretched arms, murmured reassurances and brief touches. Soon, the head paramedic, a birdlike giant with wise green eyes, turned toward them. Removing his surgical gloves, he ran a huge hand through his wiry nest of blond hair. "You wanna ride, V?"

"No, Jason. Thanks. He needs his mama more than me."

That's not true! He needs us both, Paloma wanted to cry out. But they couldn't both ride with Teddy, and already, Deanne's warm hand was urging her forward into the yawning glare of the ambulance interior. Deanne braced her elbow as she stepped clumsily up. She shivered, and Deanne handed her the leather jacket, then glanced toward Jason, pulling Pep against her side. "We'll follow you."

Jason shut one of the rear ambulance doors, but as he reached for the other, Deanne grabbed the edge of it.

"Punky."

She turned.

Deanne winked, as if to reassure her. Just like she'd done when Pep had been frightened. "I'm right behind you, P."

Paloma nodded, pulling the lapels of the jacket around her neck. The supple leather released a scent that was pure Deanne. Soap and musk, with just a touch of the vinyl polish she religiously used on the Chevelle's interior. The familiarity soothed Paloma then like Deanne's calmness had in the midst of the ordeal. What would she have done had Dee not been there? Handled it, obviously. She wasn't helpless.

Still, Deanne's reassurances, her mere presence, had kept Paloma sane in the first moments when she'd seen Teddy...pale and limp, all that blood. She shuddered, sinking into the jacket.

As the ambulance rolled, she sat next to Teddy, the memories replaying in her mind like film clips. Deanne, chin to injured chin with their son. Those oh-so-sexy crinkles around her eyes when she winked at Pep. The soft solidity and heat of her chest, the comfort of her nearness, and her lips against Paloma's hair.

All of it imbued Paloma with the strength to be courageous for Teddy and not to think of anything else.

Like the future.

Lord have mercy, she did not want to raise these sons on her own. The realization burned through her ears, deafening her like the siren's wail. The boys did need their mommy, despite what Deanne had said. She hated to admit it, but she needed Deanne, too.

❖

The first hour in the hospital was a blur. Teddy'd been unconscious for no more than two minutes, but that was long enough to warrant a battery of extra tests. An X-ray machine had been rolled into the room, and Teddy was scheduled for a CT scan. After that came a body exam, more X-rays, lab work, stitches, and cleanup. Several hours elapsed before Teddy was finished, before Paloma was convinced he'd be okay.

Much to everyone's relief, the injuries turned out to be less serious than they'd feared, though Teddy wouldn't be running through playgrounds any time soon. He'd lost five teeth—all babies—and the gash on his chin required seven stitches. His neck was stiff, and two black eyes gave him the look of a baby panda bear. The impact had bruised his chest, and his head against the swing set left him with a sizeable purple goose egg and a concussion. If that weren't enough, his palms and forearms were covered with oozy gravel burn, and his very favorite Broncos jersey had been cut off and discarded.

He was one bummed-out little guy, but at least he was going home, just as soon as the doctor returned with discharge instructions. Paloma could hardly wait. Her fear, coupled with the odor of disinfectant and the sound of Teddy's cries, had left her with a pounding headache. She could only imagine how poor Teddy felt.

Deanne, who'd been at the nurses' station calling family and friends, moved silently into the curtained area where Paloma had been sitting with the boys. She looked up, and Deanne's face warmed, which made her immediately look away. Her heart pounded and her palms grew moist.

Already she'd begun to second-guess her emotions from the ambulance. Yes, she'd been frightened. Yes, she appreciated Deanne's support. But now that the worst was over, the truth of their situation rushed back to suck her feet out from under her, like an unexpected riptide. She had been so needy, so accepting of Deanne's comfort. Fear for Teddy—that's all it was. Right?

As though the last three weeks had never occurred, Deanne slipped her hand beneath Paloma's hair to cup and massage her neck exactly how she liked it. Dee leaned in. "You okay, Punkybean?" she asked, her mouth so close she felt the caress of her breath on her cheek.

"Ah…yeah, I'm uh…" She pulled away as subtly as she could. She didn't want the boys to read into the familiarity and harbor false hope, but she didn't want to seem angry, either. Children were so damn perceptive. Though Pep appeared occupied with toys a nurse had given him, Paloma had no doubt he was attuned to every nuance of his parents' interactions. He still couldn't understand why Mommy was staying at Uncle Ruben's. More than anything, Pep just wanted them to be a family again.

"Paloma?" Deanne asked, her tone a silky caress.

Paloma crossed to the foot of the bed, then turned back toward Deanne. Determined not to allow her weakened, flip-flopped emotions make promises she wasn't sure she could keep, she tossed her hair and lifted her chin. "I'll be fine as soon as I can take Teddy home."

I.

Not we.

"Of course," Deanne murmured, but her eyes said, *So that's how it's gonna be.* Whatever bonding they'd gained at the school had been temporary, she clearly realized, and the fact that she was crushed by it all didn't escape Paloma's notice. Deanne laid her palm on Teddy's shoulder, studying his tiny sleeping form. Her chin tremored, and her nostrils flared sharply. "Thank God he's going to be okay. Poor little guy. Scared me half to death."

The show of emotion made Paloma's breath catch. God, she

felt heartless. She'd greedily taken all the comfort Deanne had offered during the ordeal, but the moment things settled down, she repaid her wife with a solid snub. Impending split aside, that wasn't the kind of person she wanted to be.

She tried to make amends for acting so selfishly with a softened tone. "How are you doing?"

"How am I?" Deanne asked, clearly still fixed on Paloma's brush-off. Her eyes narrowed, and she pursed her lips. "Not good, P. Not good at all, if you really want to know."

I meant with this, she wanted to add. *With Teddy*. "Well"—a tight swallow—"you were wonderful."

"Apparently not wonderful enough."

Paloma sighed. They were talking in riddles and subtext, but she couldn't find the right words to make it stop. Her hand snaked around the cold metal bar at the end of Teddy's bed for support.

"We'll both have different perspectives in the morning. Things'll look better then." Her gaze slid to her son.

"You think?" Deanne's voice grew husky. "Because tomorrow, and the day after, the next year, the rest of my life, Paloma, they look nothing but bleak to me."

"I was talking about Teddy."

"Yeah? Well, I think we need to talk about us."

"Not here." Her throat ached with unreleased emotion. She blinked several times. "Please."

"Then where? When? I may still be in your private purgatory for my unforgivable sins, but I know we can work through it. I'm not willing to give up." Deanne's left hand slid along the bed's side bar as she approached her, their commitment ring zinging like a long musical note against the metal.

Paloma stared down at the band Deanne hadn't yet removed, the band she hadn't removed, as a matter of fact, in the fourteen years since she'd placed it on Deanne's finger. Self-consciously, Paloma curled her bare left hand into her body, riddled with guilt. She hadn't wanted to take hers off yet, but a TV divorce therapist had suggested doing so as a symbolic first step to moving on.

So angry after the missed appointment, she'd just…reacted. She looked at Deanne's well-worn band, talons of regret gouging into her. Over and over. Clearly, Deanne wasn't moving anywhere, and part of Paloma was terrified to leave her behind.

"That's right," Deanne said, and Paloma's gaze snapped to her face. "I'm still married. *I'm* still wearing it, and I don't plan to change that. I guess I don't have as quick of an on/off switch as you."

"I don't want to talk about it now, Dee." Paloma wondered if the words were as honest as they'd once been.

"How can you say that?" Cords of muscle stood out along Deanne's neck, spanning out toward her toned shoulders. "Our marriage is the most important thing in my life."

"I meant, about the divor—" Paloma sighed and pressed two trembling fingers against her forehead, closing her eyes. Deanne knew what she meant, and she wouldn't be baited in front of the boys. She peered over at Pep again, and Deanne cupped her elbow and pulled her outside the curtains.

"He can't hear us now. No excuses."

Bitter heat ripped through her. "You know what I'm saying. The divorce, or whatever the hell we're calling it, won't just disappear because of what happened tonight. Nothing's solved. You aren't being fair—"

"Fair?" An unreadable emotion both cold and hot flashed in Deanne's eyes. She jerked her chin to the side in a restrained shrug. "Forgive me, but you know what they say about all being fair in love and war."

War? Teeth clenched, Paloma leaned in. "That's what this is now? War?"

"Absolutely not," Deanne enunciated. "God, I feel like I'm banging my head against a brick wall. This is love, Paloma Vargas. Love. Though maybe the dark side, it is still…love. We've sure as hell seen better times, but this"—she placed one palm over her own heart, the other over Paloma's—"you and me, this is *love*. Sometimes when we say 'I love you,' we forget it *isn't* a simple thing, or a sentiment we can take for granted. Remember those words?"

Paloma fumed. How dared Deanne throw their vows in her face. She stepped back from Deanne's touch. "What about cherish?" she snapped. "Did you forget that one?" Spinning away, she reached up and caressed her temples, trying to quash the burst of bitterness. Long moments passed, during which Paloma felt every hot pulse of blood through her veins.

"Did I, Punky?" came Deanne's emotionally shredded reply.

Paloma turned back.

Deanne didn't appear angry. She looked crestfallen. "Because if my actions didn't show how much I cherished you, I swear, I didn't intend—" She cut herself off and fought for the right words. "I never knew you felt that way."

Paloma hadn't expected that, and for a moment, didn't know what to say. How could Deanne not have known? The silences and conspicuous absences. The disappointments, the distance. Working all the time. How could Paloma have been the only one to see it?

She reached up and wound her fingers in the chain of the diamond pendant Deanne had bought her when Pep was born. *Tell her*, Paloma's mind whispered. *Now or never*.

"Yeah, you did forget. You forgot the word, the vow, and most of all, you forgot *me*. That's the one thing I can't live with."

"I never meant to make you feel as if I forgot you." Deanne's eyes melted with sincerity. "If it didn't show, Jesus, I'm so incredibly sorry. But give me a chance to change."

"Yet another chance?" Paloma scoffed, but it felt forced.

"Yes, Punky. And another, and another, until I fumble through and get it right. Yes. Same as I'd do for you. Aren't we worth it?" Deanne waited, but Paloma didn't answer. "I was showing you love the only way I knew how, P. Doing my pathetic best. I didn't know I was failing you." She let her arms fall at her sides. "Can't you see that?"

Paloma tried to shake the confusion from her head. "I d-don't know. Didn't the distance bother you, too, or are you able to survive in an emotional vacuum?"

The skin tightened across Deanne's prominent cheekbones. Pain-shadowed eyes searched her face. "Maybe I'm less emotionally insightful than you, but I never intentionally forgot you or our sons. Every day I get up and go to work, every overtime minute I spend away from home is for you and our boys. It's how I show my love, being the kind of partner my mother never had with Victor. Honestly, I thought you knew that much about me."

Paloma squeezed her eyes shut, blocking out the rush of tenderness. Damnit, she had known that, somewhere along the line. Was she wrong about the split? If so, why did she hurt so much? "Please don't say any more. I don't want to fight. It's been a rough night—" Her words caught, and she covered her mouth with her hand. She couldn't bear Dee's remorse now, on top of her confusion and the terror over Teddy's accident. She felt a light hand on her forehead, Deanne's palm smoothing down her cheek.

"It's been rough—for all of us. But we hung together, like always." Deanne placed a soft kiss on Paloma's hairline. "I'll do anything to make things better, Punky, except end things without a fight. When I told my mother about the separation, do you know what she said?"

Paloma's heart took a sickening plunge. "What?"

"She said, 'Don't lose the best thing life ever gave you, *m'ija*. Ruben's better off without that Merrilee, but Paloma is a gem. Go get your family back, whatever it takes.'" Deanne paused, searching Paloma's face. When she spoke again, her voice was hoarse. "Mother knows best. You've got to forgive me for the damned appointment, for all of it. Give me a chance."

Paloma waved the plea away, trying not to focus on Rosario's heartbreakingly sweet words, on the warmth, the embrace of family. "What you don't seem to understand is this: if you hurt me again, I would shatter. I can't take the risk."

Deanne's hand snaked around her wrist, and she lifted Paloma's fingers to her lips. "I won't hurt you"—a kiss on her palm—"if you help me to realize when I'm doing something stupid. Don't grin and bear it, be honest with me. Help me."

"I"—she sighed—"Deanne."

Deanne released her hand, but pulled her into an embrace that was more desperate than tender. Paloma couldn't make herself move away. Dee's hand cupped the back of her head, smoothed her hair, her heartbeat strong and steady against Paloma's cheek. "I know we can work, P. Say you know it, too."

"I...I don't know." She stiffened in the hold, but her words had no oomph. "Please. I can't deal with this now, on top of everything else."

Deanne's arms slackened, and Paloma extracted herself. Stepping away, she shored up her dignity, smoothing her grass-stained clothing. "Let's focus on Teddy now."

Dee's eyes shone unusually bright in her haggard face. But her voice—that was the worst. Forlorn and imploring. "I am thinking about him. And his brother, and how much they need their parents—"

"Mommy?" Teddy croaked, his voice was no more than a dry whisper from the other side of the curtain. After a split second-pause during which she studied Paloma's face, Deanne brushed aside the curtain to go to her son.

Paloma remained outside and willed her adrenaline to dissipate. As the sounds of their soft murmurs reached her ears, she backed against the wall and slumped, closing her eyes. Her resistance to Deanne was slipping away. Sand through fingers.

Dared she believe an apology—another empty promise perhaps—might have the strength to correct the massive structural damage to their marriage? But Deanne had offered so much more than a simple "I'm sorry."

A seedling of doubt took root in Paloma's heart, and she bit her lip. Suppose Deanne truly hadn't known how unhappy she'd been. As her disillusionment had mounted, things had just grown quieter and quieter in their home until the silence became painful and deafening. Until she couldn't bear to hear *nothing* anymore.

A shudder ran through her, and she wrapped her arms around her torso to stave off the soul-deep cold. Would she ever be warm again? Realizing she still wore Deanne's soft jacket, redolent with her scent and softly shaped to her body, she slipped her thumbs up under the lapels. She lifted the leather to her face and indulged in one more long breath of her wife's essence before she reluctantly shrugged it off to give it back. That scent, she knew, would chase her to her grave. With choking indecision like a tightly bound gag in her mouth, she pushed aside the curtain and joined her bedraggled family.

Deanne's head came up as she neared. "Teddy wants to know if I'll be staying with him tonight." Dee's searching eyes conveyed so much more than the words that formed the simple statement.

Oh, God. She didn't know if she could resist Deanne's comfort if they slept beneath the same roof. She opened her mouth to protest when Teddy's rough little plea stopped her.

"Please, Mama."

Her heart wrenched. Teddy needed his mommy, and *she* was just being selfish. She peered at Deanne again, chewing the inside of her cheek. It shocked her to realize how much she wanted Deanne there. For Teddy. Now wasn't the time to worry about anything other than her little injured boy. She placed her hand gently on Teddy's tummy and smiled. "Of course, Teddy bear. We'll all be there together—me, you, Mommy, and Pep."

CHAPTER SIX

Addendum to Paloma Vargas's journal entry, Monday, September 24

The house is dark except for the glow of Teddy's night-light next to me here on the floor. I can't sleep. Deanne and I are taking turns looking in on Teddy, but I figured as long as I was lying there staring at the ceiling, I might as well come listen to my baby's breathing.

Thank God Teddy's safe. Still, the trial isn't over. A second concussion within the next couple weeks could be very serious, the doctor said. It will be a full-time job keeping Teddy inactive that long.

Deanne's here. Two rooms over.

It should be normal, but it's not.

What could I say to an injured little boy's pleas for his mommy? No? To tell you the truth, it's a relief to share this fear, this responsibility for keeping Teddy safe. We have to wake him every two hours and ask him a bunch of questions, just to make sure he's coherent. I'm terrified that the next time I go to wake him, it won't work, or I'll sleep through my alarm, or that I'll lose the battle against my weakness and return to the guest room bed with Deanne, just to feel her warmth surround me, her fingers slip inside me. God.

Me <———wimp.

I can't sleep for wanting to feel her. Having Deanne home, but in another room, is awful. I miss her. I'll admit it. So damn much that sometimes I feel like I can't breathe. I still don't know if we can work things out, but what if, for the boys' sake, we start by being friends? Isn't that how we started in the first place? Oops, someone's coming.

Paloma managed to scramble to her feet just as the door began to squeak on its hinges. Expecting Deanne, she held her breath and her journal equally tight as the golden cone of light spilled into the dark room. But it was Pep, not Deanne, who shadowed the doorway. His belly stuck out, and he rubbed one eye with the back of his hand, just like he'd done since he was a toddler.

"Mama?" he croaked.

She set the notebook aside and went to him, pulling him against her. "Shh, what's the matter, honey?"

"I had a bad dream 'bout Teddy." He flickered a worried glance at his brother's twin bed. "Is he okay?"

"Sure, beetle bug." She smiled to reassure him, then urged him into the room. "Want to come see?"

Pep nodded. They crept to Teddy's bedside, and Pep peered over, holding his breath until his battered little brother blew out a quivery-lipped exhale. A mischievous smile brightened Pep's face, and he scrunched his shoulders and peered up at Paloma. She tilted her head toward the door. They tiptoed out of the room and into Pep's.

When she had him all tucked in, she sat on his bed and rubbed his chest, loving him so much it took her a moment to speak. She didn't want him to hold his emotions in. Reaching out, she smoothed his pajama top, then she stretched out beside him, propping herself up on one elbow. Pep nestled against her. "Want a story?"

"Naw. Just stay here for a little bit."

"Okay." She indulged in the pleasure of cradling her son, considering he was at the age where he didn't allow it all the time. When Pep's body had relaxed, she cleared her throat. "That was pretty scary tonight, huh?"

"Yeah. Lotsa blood."

"Now you know why I'm always nagging you yard monkeys not to run." She tickled him, and he squirmed and giggled. A moment later he fell silent again. "What are you thinking about, Pep?"

"Stuff."

"What stuff, *m'ijo*?"

Round, solemn eyes rose to implore hers. "Does Mommy get to come home now for real? She said she was sorry, and you always say it's not good to hold a crutch."

She swallowed thickly. "Grudge."

"Yeah, a grudge."

Her stomach contracted. *Damn.* Pep had heard them arguing at the hospital. She sighed. "It's not as simple as that…but I don't want you to worry about—"

"But why not?" His voice wobbled, and his eyes filled with moisture. "We're a family, and she 'pologized. It should be simple. It should be *that* simple. She's my mommy. I don't wanna divorce her."

"Oh, sweetheart, you won't ever div—" She sighed, sickened over Pep's anguish and hopelessly inept at easing it. "Listen. She'll always be your mommy. No matter what."

"But I want her here. I miss her every day, Mama. I love her."

"I—" *Love her, too*, she was about to say. She bit her lip, hating that Pep was troubled. "I know you do, Pep. She loves you, too. And so do I."

"But do you love Mommy?"

She looked away, plucking at a yarn tie on Pep's quilt. Her eldest son always cut to the chase. He wanted to know *what* he wanted to know, *when* he wanted to know it. Period. Such her little man.

"Do you, Mama? Because families are 'sposed to love each other."

He'd know if she lied. "Of course I do, bug."

Pep flapped his arms as if Paloma were the worst kind of idiot. "So why don't you just tell her that so we can be a family again? In this house, like always."

Sadness took hold at his simplistic view of things. She kissed his forehead. "This is between me and your mommy. I don't want you to worry"—she tapped his nose—"okay? No matter what, we're still your mama and mommy, and we love you to pieces. Now go to sleep."

"Okay," he said grudgingly.

She waited until he'd snuggled down, until his eyelids grew heavy, then rose and walked to the door, switching off his light. Her eyes adjusted to the dim orange glow from his racecar night-light.

As she was closing the door, Pep stopped her. "Mama?"

"Yes?" For a moment, she wondered if she imagined he'd called her. When he finally spoke, she could barely hear him.

"*I* cherish you," he whispered. "Can that be enough so Mommy can come home? Please?"

Awed and humbled, she leaned her cheek against the edge of the door and stared through the darkness at the wonderful little soul she was so lucky to have as a son. She carefully sidestepped his question. "Honey," she said, on a sigh. "I cherish you, too."

In the moments before wakefulness took grasp, Deanne imagined the breakup had been a bad dream. She heard Paloma's gentle words, smelled her spicy-sweet skin, and figured Paloma was waking her to make love, like she'd used to do. God, Deanne loved her supple body. Even more so since childbirth had left a few marks, like beautiful badges of honor. They only served to make her more womanly in Deanne's eyes, softer and more enticing. *Mine alone.*

Eyes closed in decadent drowsiness, Deanne rolled toward the sound of Paloma's voice and reached out, thrilled when her palm made contact with her lush, round breast. She heard Paloma gasp, and a smile curved Deanne's lips. One of the best things about Paloma was her lack of vocal inhibition. Deanne never had to wonder what Paloma wanted or liked—she made it abundantly clear, and that was so goddamned sexy.

Dee kneaded Paloma's soft flesh, the moan low and rough in her throat. Paloma's nipple hardened against her hand, and her body reacted in a rush of heat and tightness. "I want to be inside you, baby girl." Deanne pulled her closer. "Let me feel you—"

Something like a handcuff clamped Dee's wrist, stopping the wicked caress. "Deanne!" came Paloma's voice. Raspy. Stern.

Deanne frowned and squinted, just in time to see Paloma shove her hand away. Dee's eyes snapped open fully as Paloma backed toward the door.

Lurching up so quickly it brought stars to her vision, Deanne scrubbed her hands over her face and fought for her bearings. The guest room. Reality struck like a punch to the solar plexus. Oh yeah. "Paloma. Baby, I-I'm sorry. I was dreaming."

A flare of...awareness sapped the shuttered look from Paloma's eyes. Making no move to leave, no move to come closer, she crossed her arms over her chest and moistened her lips with a nervous flick of her tongue. "It's your turn."

God, Dee slept too heavily. Must have something to do with being home, in a bed that didn't feel like a medieval torture device. Something to do with being between sheets that smelled like...Paloma's fabric softener.

Damn. *Teddy!*

Immediately sobered, Deanne ripped back the covers and swung her feet to the floor, reaching up to rub her eyes. "Shoot. Did I oversleep?"

"No—" Paloma started forward, then stopped, and Dee realized she was wearing sleep boxers…and nothing else. The telltale wash of color rose up Paloma's neck, and her gaze fluttered away. She felt the wanting, too. Deanne could see it all over her like a full-body tattoo. For now, she'd leave it alone. *For now.*

With a deep breath, Paloma raised her gaze. "He's fine. I woke him half an hour ago. But I thought I'd try and get some sleep…"

"Yeah, of course. You go on." Deanne crossed to the chair in the corner to retrieve the T-shirt she'd shed earlier. She wouldn't normally cover her bare chest in front of her wife, but things were different now. Paloma clearly didn't want to see her naked body. As Dee pulled the wear-softened cotton over her head, she tried to wash the night-blurred images of Paloma, the dream feel of her body from her mind.

"You want me to make you some coffee?"

Always so thoughtful, her Paloma. Even now. "You don't have to wait on me. I've told you that before."

"Yes, but your coffee sucks."

Dee chuckled softly. "True. I'm fine, though. Go on to bed."

She would've thought Paloma would take advantage of the opportunity to flee, but instead, she leaned against the doorjamb, feet crossed. Deanne's gaze dropped to those damned ridiculous cow slippers Paloma so dearly loved, and she bit the inside corner of her mouth to keep from smiling. "Something on your mind?"

"Pep heard us."

Deanne frowned. "Come again?"

"At the hospital. Pep heard us talking." She swept her hair into a loose ponytail and held it. Deanne tried not to notice the little tendril curls that escaped to dance against her neck. "He said, 'I cherish you, Mama. Can that be enough so Mommy can come home?'"

"Jesus," Deanne said, on an exhale.

Paloma pressed her lips in a line. "I don't want him thinking he can control things, Dee. That this is, in any way, his fault. It's too big a burden for a little boy." She released a small growl. "I'd hoped this separation wouldn't affect them."

Even as she tried to repress it, Deanne could feel gaping disbelief on her face. "You're kidding, right?"

"No." Paloma gave a few fluttery blinks and her chin jutted stubbornly. "Our relationship is between us, not them."

"Baby, they're our sons. Take it from me, children become an unwitting part of any relationship problems." Deanne moved closer, drawn by the softness of Paloma. Unable to resist, she reached out and ran the backs of her fingers down the silk of Paloma's cheek. Paloma didn't pull back, but Deanne watched her neck move with a tight swallow. "There's nothing we can do about it if you insist on a legal split."

"You're just trying to make me feel guilty."

"No, I'm being realistic." Dee tried to lighten her tone, because the sight of Paloma in the doorway, forlorn and torn and chewing her lip, sprang a well of compassion inside her. "If you go through with this, you'll live here. I'll live somewhere else. It's called a *broken* home. Broken." Dee let that sink in. "You understand the implications of that, right?"

"Yeah, but we can make sure it doesn't…affect them," Paloma offered, seeming none too sure of herself.

God, Deanne wanted to hold her. Or shake some sense into her. "Punky—" Hands on her hips, Deanne hung her head and expelled a breath. Her words would hurt Paloma, and she hated that. More than anything, she wanted to repair things between them. Why did it seem so fucking impossible at every turn? "It will affect them. I'm not saying it'll destroy them, but joint custody, splitting their time between two houses—I'm sorry. It will affect them. It's a fact." Deanne toyed with the wisdom of going on. Screw it. Paloma needed to hear the ugly truth. "If you insist on breaking up our family, that's a by-product you'll have to accept."

A maelstrom of emotions crossed Paloma's face. Guilt, indecision, anger, futility. Finally she slid her back down the wall until she sat on the ground. "Damnit, why does this have to be so difficult?"

Paloma wasn't a weeper, yet Deanne could tell she was way past due for a good cry. But she knew Punky well enough to realize she'd die before letting anyone see what she'd perceive as weakness. *Her mother's daughter.*

Deanne shook her head, filled with a tangle of frustration and tenderness. If only Paloma would express her dissatisfaction instead of letting it fester. She needed to learn that Deanne didn't expect her to smile prettily and endure a life with which she was unhappy. But Deanne also wanted Paloma to realize she didn't have to cold-turkey end things to find that elusive happiness, and if she did choose that path, there were repercussions. "Because it is difficult, P. It's a life-changing decision for all of us."

Paloma's stoic silence tore at Deanne's heart. Part of her wanted to wrap Paloma in an embrace. Another wanted to force her to see how wrong this was for all of them. But instead, Deanne grudgingly told Paloma what *she* needed to hear. Just this once.

"Look, it's going to be okay." Dee nudged her arm until she lifted her dry, drawn face, then offered her hand. Paloma took it, and Dee pulled her straight up into a hug, rocking her side to side. "We'll figure it out for the boys, Paloma. I won't lie—you'll never convince me splitting up is for the best—"

"I don't want to ar—"

"Shh." Dee pressed warm fingers gently against Paloma's luscious lips. "I'm not trying to argue. Hear me out."

Paloma's body stiffened. Held. Relaxed.

"From now on, we'll work out what we can for the boys. That's all I'm saying. Okay? I don't want them hurt either."

Paloma's hackles lowered. "But they will be hurt."

A beat passed. "I'd say they probably already are."

The shuddering sigh Paloma expelled seemed to deplete her of energy. "Jesus Christ, I'm a terrible, selfish mother."

"Don't be ridiculous. The boys worship you. Now, come on. You're exhausted." Deanne tucked an arm around her and steered her to the hallway. "It's been one hell of a day. You need some rest."

Defeated, Paloma shuffled next to Deanne. Their cadence was off, and she jostled under Deanne's arm with every step as though they were sluggish participants in a three-legged race. Deanne's lips twisted ruefully. How symbolic. Walking next to each other through life, yet hearing wildly different beats. But were they, really? Or did one of them just have two left feet?

When Deanne had settled Paloma into bed—their bed—she reluctantly backed off. There'd be time for discussion...and hopefully more...when Paloma wasn't exhausted almost to the point of incoherence.

They murmured good nights, and Deanne turned to leave, but in the doorway, she stopped. What had Sgt. Obermeyer said about women needing more than what she'd, apparently, always given Paloma? She stared through the semidarkness at Paloma's tiny form. "How about I bring you some of that tea you like? It'll relax you. Help you sleep."

Paloma's liquid brown eyes warmed, cautiously, hopefully. "If you don't mind. That'd be really nice." She pulled the comforter up around her chest and pressed it down with her arms, looking almost embarrassed by the offer. "Thanks."

Deanne's smile came slowly. "Baby girl, it's my pleasure."

Ten minutes later, Deanne carried the steaming tea back down the hall and paused to check the boys before taking it in to Paloma. She peeked in on Pep first—sleeping soundly. Next stop, Teddy's room. Deanne set the cup on the bureau and crossed over, angling her head as she peered down on her black-and-blue son. She placed her palm on Teddy's scraped-up tummy.

Teddy stirred, then opened his eyes. "Mommy..."

"Hey, little man." Deanne tucked the quilt Grandma had made for Teddy when he was a baby. "How're you feeling?"

Teddy's eyelids drooped, and he made little chewing motions before murmuring, "Head hurts."

I'll bet. "You know why?"

He shifted beneath the patchwork, settling into a tight fetal position, his back to Deanne. "I fell at the school," came his sleep-slurred answer. "'Cuz I was runnin' and Mama says not to run."

Deanne's heart expanded, and she smiled. "It's okay to run, *hijito*, as long as you watch where you're going."

"And those doctors cut my Broncos jersey."

A soft laugh lifted Deanne's shoulders, and love filled her chest. "We'll get you a new jersey, don't worry. Go to sleep, buddy." But the suggestion was unnecessary. Teddy was out cold.

As Deanne turned to retrieve the teacup, the night-light illuminated cover of Paloma's journal grabbed her attention. *Read me*, it whispered seductively. Dee stood at-gunpoint still, heart pounding with warning. What in the hell? In almost two decades, she had never invaded Paloma's privacy. Paloma had hundreds of journals stored somewhere in this house, and Deanne had never so much as cracked a single binding.

But there it was.

Beckoning.

If she could just get a little bit into Paloma's head, get some kind of handle on where she stood...

No. It wasn't right. Deanne threw a guilty glance over her shoulder and clasped her fingers together behind her neck. Did she dare?

The journal drew her again. She tugged at the bottom of her T-shirt and crossed her arms. Then...uncrossed them. Busy movement. Ridiculous. She moved toward the journal as if she were stalking it. Squatting, she lifted the sleek red notebook and smoothed her palm over the buttery leather cover.

Yes?

No?

This was one of those no-turning-back moments, like committing a crime.

Once she'd crossed the line, no going back. Period. Her seventeen-year record of never having invaded Paloma's privacy would be forever lost.

Worth the risk?

She fanned the page edges thoughtfully…considering. Hadn't she claimed all was fair in love and war? If the key to winning Paloma back was inked on the pages of this book and Dee didn't look, she'd never forgive herself. Ruben told her to do whatever it took.

All's fair.

Desperate times called for desperate measures. What other clichés could she apply to rationalize her actions?

A jolt of nerves lifted her gaze to the door once, then fully committed, she released a tense breath and opened the book. Damnit, she wanted her wife back. She didn't know where else to look for answers, and Paloma certainly wasn't offering any. *What do I have to lose?*

Deanne crept silently into the master bedroom. Paloma's back was turned toward her, the profile of her body an inviting, womanly undulation beneath the comforter. For a moment Dee thought Paloma might have drifted off. But when she set the teacup on the nightstand, Paloma's movement rustled the sheets and her eyes found Deanne's.

Her skin looked velvety in the golden lamp glow. Wavy auburn hair spilled over the pillow, and her eyelids drooped drowsily. The down comforter had tugged her silk nightgown tightly against her breasts, and Deanne couldn't make herself look away. Such aching beauty. The mother of their sons.

She feared she couldn't speak, but then Paloma scooted up and sat against the brass headboard pipes, breaking the spell.

Deanne gestured toward the cup. "Your tea, milady."

"You found the tea bags and everything. Wow." Paloma tucked her hair behind those ears Deanne loved to nibble and reached for the cup, blowing steam off the front as she held it. Her round, wary eyes tracked Deanne's movements. In between blowing, she cleared the sleepiness from her throat. "What took you so long?"

"I checked the boys. Hung out for a bit." Deanne sat on the end of the bed, smiling in a way she hoped would convey her unspoken, secret agreement—being friends was a good place to start. Dee's heart soared remembering the words of confusion and desire Paloma had written. Deep inside, Paloma wanted Dee to navigate her way back into her heart…and she would. That was all Deanne needed to know.

"Everything okay?" She still hadn't sipped the tea.

"Yeah. Pep's out cold and Teddy woke up to talk to me."

"Good. What did he say?"

"He said he got hurt at school because he was running and 'Mama says not to run.'"

Paloma laughed. "At least some of my nagging is sinking in. That's a good sign." As though their easy camaraderie had taken her by surprise, she blinked and let her gaze flutter down into the cup.

"I added one sugar cube and a big squirt of lemon juice."

One eyebrow arched, and she took a sip. "Mmm. Thanks. I didn't realize you knew how I liked it."

Deanne eased closer and sat cross-legged beside Paloma, striving to read her body language. She didn't want to push. "I knew. But I should've taken advantage of that knowledge more often." She paused. "I'm sorry."

A tension-wrought chasm of the unsaid stretched between them. Their eyes locked. Deanne couldn't tear herself away. God help her, she didn't want to leave. The moment took on a surreal quality that entranced Deanne, as though death had stolen her love, and this was but her filmy ghost come to pay one last visit. She had so much to say, so much regret. She feared if she looked away, Paloma would disappear, and where would Deanne be then? "Paloma…"

She said nothing at first, but Deanne watched her, unable to take a full breath. As she twisted to set the cup on the saucer, Dee admired the expanse of smooth caramel skin that showed above the deep V-back of her gown, desperately wanting to touch it.

She faced her again. "Deanne?"

"Yes?"

Her hands smoothed the comforter covering her lap in a wide arc. "C-can you do something for me," she whispered, "without reading too much into it? Three things, actually." She nibbled the corner of her mouth, clearly uncertain.

Deanne's heart leapt. "Anything, baby girl. Absolutely anything."

"I want to hold off on mediation for a while. All this with Teddy…it just isn't practical."

Stunned, Deanne almost forgot to answer. "Of course. Yes. Whatever you say." A pause. "What else?"

"Will you"—she blinked worriedly—"stay for the week and help me with Teddy?"

"You don't even have to ask." Deanne's heart began to drum. "Request number three?"

Looking dubious and needy and morose, she dragged back the covers, exposing her legs, bare beneath the hem of her gown. "Will you hold me?" Her voice faltered. "Just for tonight?"

Not just for tonight, love. Forever. Deanne wanted to say it, but she didn't, determined to let Paloma take the lead in this blind man's bluff game of finding their way back to each other. She crawled up the bedcovers, her motions languid. "I'll hold you as much as you want me to, Punky. For as long as you want me to."

Deanne slid between the sheets and molded her body to the

back of Paloma's, tucking her head closer. Her hair smelled like home and heaven, and her skin slipped against Deanne's like an elusive memory. She combed Paloma's tumbled curls back from her forehead and kissed her there, on her ear, and on the side of her neck. "Sleep, P. Teddy's okay, and I'm here. Everything will be fine, I promise."

A sigh shuddered from Paloma as the tension left her body. Then, almost silently, she began to cry.

"Hey, now," Deanne soothed, wanting to comfort her, but glad she was finally releasing all that pent-up emotion. She settled for snuggling closer, rocking Paloma gently.

"D-don't tell me not to cry." Her voice was high-pitched, squeaky from the tears.

"Never crossed my mind."

"I'm not some weak, helpless female, but m-my son is h-hurt. My life is a horrible m-mess. Don't you dare t-tell me."

One corner of Deanne's mouth lifted with acute tenderness. Paloma sounded ready to punch her if she tried to shush the tears. "You go on and cry, P. Nothing weak about that. Let it out." Dee continued smoothing the curls slowly back from Paloma's temple and watched them spring back into place beneath her palm. A shot of 100 proof, unadulterated love burned her throat. She would do anything for this woman. Anything. "I'll just hold you. Okay?"

Paloma nodded, her chest hiking with quick little inhales. Deanne cradled her tightly. As the tears seeped from the corners of her eyes, she watched Paloma press her lips together in a valiant effort to control them. Her tummy contracted and trembled beneath Deanne's palm. Every few moments, she blew out air and hiccuped more in.

"God, I fucking h-hate crying."

Deanne chuckled softly. "Yeah, I think I know that about you by now." The dim room smelled like her perfume and lemony tea, like green apple shampoo and woman. All the details she'd grown so accustomed to in the past fourteen years stood out in brash focus. Paloma—her wife, her *life*—had never felt more right in Deanne's arms.

Paloma reached up and brushed tear trails from her ears, then whipped Deanne a staccato glance before settling her head back into the crook of her shoulder and releasing a miserable sigh. Taking a little gulp of air, she whispered, "Deanne…babe, I'm sorry."

Nervous hope jolted inside Dee. She worked hard to tamp down her thundering emotion before speaking. Swallowing once, she planted a kiss on her wife's bare shoulder. "For what?"

"For not telling you. Not…t-talking to you. I don't know." Paloma shifted in Deanne's embrace until she could look up into her face, and Deanne read contrition and vulnerability in her expression. "For letting things get worse and worse until there was just no turning back."

Deanne smiled, loving Paloma so much, she shook with it. "There's always a place to turn back, and you don't have to apologize. I'm sorry I didn't ask you what was wrong. It's not my way, but I want to change. I will change. I'll—" Her words caught on thick emotion, and she clenched her jaw, fighting for control. "I'll do whatever it takes to be the woman you want, if you'll just let me."

Paloma's wet eyes searched Deanne's face for a long time, and then she sighed. "You've always been the woman I want, Dee. Don't change too much." The words were a husky warble, an admission that had been difficult for her to make, Deanne was sure.

She didn't know what to say.

In slow increments, Paloma stilled, except for her chest above the plunging neckline of her nightgown. It rose and fell, rapidly at first, then gradually shallowing until Deanne could detect small tremors of anticipation on her dusky rose flesh. The diamond pendant Dee had given her when Pep made his squalling entrance into the world lay nestled in her shadowy cleavage. It rolled slightly with each hitched inhale and exhale. The room hummed with the pent-up desire between them, with the need, the sorrow, the desperation, the fear.

"Whatever you want. Whatever it takes." Deanne's body responded to their fiery connection, and she wondered if Paloma felt the throbbing heat against her. Wondered if it excited her, made her want Deanne as much as Deanne wanted her. "It can be okay if we want it to be."

Dee waited.

Paloma didn't offer up any denials.

Blood pounded in Deanne's neck as she marveled at the sheer, promising stillness of the moment. She dipped her head closer, testing, knowing if Paloma pulled back, she'd die inside. Deanne closed the distance with achingly slow movements. Paloma never pulled back.

Her gaze fluttered from Deanne's eyes to her mouth just as she raked that plump bottom lip between her teeth. A simple gesture, yet powerful and telling. It completely undid Deanne.

With a groan from some sheltered feminine well deep inside, Deanne leaned forward and captured Paloma's lips. Her lemon-scented breath rushed gently forth, and Deanne drank it in, wanting to consume her, to meld with her. She kissed, nipped, loved her mouth and felt a hot stinging at the back of her eyes when Paloma returned the attention with fervor. Her small, capable hands found their way under the T-shirt Deanne had worn only out of respect for her, and her abdominal muscles contracted at the cool touch on her overheated skin. Paloma's hands slid deftly up Deanne's torso to cup her breasts, thumbs brushing her nipples with confidence. The reminder of the old Paloma prompted a sharp hiss from Deanne. Desire swelled and burst inside her.

Paloma explored Deanne's taut breasts with hungry palms, caressing and pressing, grazing Dee's flesh with the pads of her fingers. Her hands smoothed around to Deanne's back, and the embrace pillowed their breasts together. As Dee's tongue explored

Paloma's mouth, she reveled in the feeling of silk over tightened nipples, Paloma's softer curves molding against her firmer, muscular form. Swollen and pulsating, Deanne surrendered to the urge to spread Paloma's legs with one thigh and thrust. Paloma rewarded Dee with a moan, a suggestive turn toward her, a restless tug of her nightgown so they could be skin-on-skin.

Astonishment ripped through Deanne. An agreement? Could it be?

Deanne's flat palm smoothed a route from shoulder to hip as she lifted her mouth from hers. "Paloma…"

"No, please." Her eyelids fluttered shut and she licked her lips. "Don't talk. Not now."

Warning stabbed at Dee, but she was too far gone. She cupped one side of Paloma's face and delved into her hot, inviting mouth once again, thumb tracing the curve of her cheekbone. Could Paloma only bear to make love to Dee if she didn't think about it? If they didn't talk about it?

No. Deanne couldn't abide that. She had to know Paloma loved and wanted her as much as she wanted Paloma, and not just physically.

Maneuvering over Paloma's small body, Dee raised her thigh higher, until her flesh met searing wetness. She rocked, and Paloma writhed, arching higher to the taunting pressure Deanne knew she loved. She pulled her head back and watched Paloma's passion, her heart thudding. *Let me please you*, she thought as her thigh muscle flexed with the rhythm against Paloma's body. She wanted to make Paloma come, needed to know she still could.

Eyes closed, Paloma arched her head back and released a small moan. The wellspring of raw need inside Deanne gushed. She propped herself on one elbow and hooked her other hand under the hem of her T-shirt, yanking it over her head.

"Take your clothes off, baby," Deanne said, in a purr.

Paloma didn't hesitate.

Deanne's eyes devoured Paloma as she tossed the shirt across the room, then shed her sleep boxers just as unceremoniously.

Before she had the chance to settle back against her wife's body, Paloma's hand snaked between them and slid into Deanne's wet, hot desire.

Dee groaned, leaning her head on the pillow next to Paloma's temple as Paloma pushed into her. Again. And again. And again.

Confident.

Hungry.

Demanding.

A ragged moan broke loose from Deanne's chest and she undulated her body in sync with Paloma's rhythm.

"More."

Another finger. A deeper push.

"No, *more.*"

Paloma gave her exactly what she wanted, what she hadn't even realized she needed, until she felt so full, so tight around Paloma's hand, she'd never experience that aching emptiness again. Dee thought she might die from the acute pleasure, but *damn*, what a way to go.

Paloma reached her free arm around Deanne's hips and held her tightly against the thrusting, expertly using her thumb to caress Deanne's deepest throb. Their moans and gasps and scent filled the room. It wasn't humanly possible to get as close to Paloma as Deanne wanted, but she wanted her so fully inside. All the way.

"Harder."

"Roll over."

"No," Dee gasped. "Like this. Just like…this." She rose up and lifted her hips into Paloma's hand hard, harder, until she knew she was going to explode, until she knew she couldn't hold on. "Jesus, baby—"

"Let go, Dee. Let me love you like this."

Deanne folded over Paloma as her body spasmed inside, clenching and releasing, so utterly wet. Her thighs trembled, her breaths stalled. The tears she'd held back for so long came forth, and she buried her face in Paloma's neck and did exactly as she was told. She let go.

Paloma sighed, her body relaxing in barely perceptible increments.

Several heartbeats passed. Deanne sighed. "Don't even think about it."

"What?" Paloma asked, sliding her hand out of Deanne's body and massaging the moisture over her center.

"I am nowhere near done with you."

Paloma's husky laugh resonated against Deanne's chest, stoking the fire again. Dee rained kisses on her collarbone and chest, tugging Paloma's nipples into her mouth with her lips and tongue and teeth as she cupped her breasts, lifting them like a starving woman. Paloma arched into Deanne's mouth, groaning and twisting. Her musky, sexually aroused scent wafted up to tease and entice Deanne lower. Deanne kissed the salty perspiration from between Paloma's breasts as her thumbs brushed and teased her pearled nipples. She could scarcely think for the throbbing urgency to taste Paloma, to be inside her, to feel her come against her tongue and around her hand. It was a pure, singular need that eclipsed the rest of the world.

Smoothing her way up the insides of Paloma's arms, Deanne guided her wife's hands to the bars of the headboard and curved them around the posts, covering them with her own. Deanne gazed into Paloma's eyes, then forced herself to stop touching, kissing, moving. She went completely still until Paloma's eyes opened. She blinked up with a sweet combination of trepidation, vulnerability and drugging desire.

"I'm going to make love to you," Deanne half whispered, half growled. "Tell me now if that isn't what you want, P, and I'll stop."

Paloma didn't answer, but Dee saw her shudder and felt the goose bumps on her skin. She slid her hands from Paloma's shoulders, over her breasts, down her stomach, and around to the soft, round flesh of her ass. Paloma's eyes drifted closed again as Deanne gently raised her, kissing and nipping and licking at her inner thighs, her tummy—everywhere except where she knew Paloma wanted her mouth most. Paloma was ready for her; she could see it, could feel the heat of her. Deanne's mouth tingled with desire. But she wanted Paloma's mind and heart ready as well as her body.

Dee would taste her…but first—

She sat back on her knees. "Paloma. Baby girl, look at me."

Paloma's eyelids raised to half-mast, and she leaned her cheek against her upstretched arm, hands white-knuckled on the iron slats above her head.

Deanne smiled gently, then reached up and placed her fingers in Paloma's mouth. Paloma groaned and sucked, bucking her body up toward Deanne.

Slipping her wet fingers from Paloma's hot mouth, Deanne positioned them just at the opening between her legs. "Look at me when I make love to you, P. I need you to see the love in my eyes. I have to know you want it, too."

Paloma's chest rose and fell, her mouth slightly parted. After a moment, she moistened her lips with a flick of her tongue, and her eyelids drooped with provocative shyness. "I'm watching, lover."

A tangled blast of pain and desire and connection and loss ripped through Deanne's chest, blurring the moment. Paloma hadn't called her that in forever. With one solid thrust of desire and possession and need, Deanne drive into Paloma until her thighs strained. She cried out, and Dee leaned forward to cover Paloma's small body, bracing her forearm beneath Paloma's back as she fucked her—confident, fervent, so…*so* in love. Deanne wanted to leave no doubt in Paloma's mind—they belonged together. Paloma began to clench and spasm around her, and Deanne's breath caught. She looked up. Paloma's eyes were closed. *No. Not yet.* "Look at me," Dee rasped through labored breaths. "Baby, open your eyes."

She did.

Locking their gazes, Deanne leveraged into Paloma's body, hard, harder, faster. Through passion-clenched teeth, she grunted, "I won't let you go, Paloma. I can't. No one else will ever be inside you like this—" Hot tears blurred Deanne's eyes as Paloma's body gripped fiercely. The power of her impending release nearly blinded Dee.

"Not yet."

"Dee, please…"

"No."

Paloma gritted her teeth, shuddering against Deanne's thrusts again and again. Dee drank in the sight of Paloma's chest flushing almost purple with tension, her nipples puckering pebble hard as the goose bumps washed down her body. So hot. So tight.

Her tears fell in glistening splatters on Paloma's heated flesh. When that internal quake began to peak, Deanne pulled out and took Paloma into her mouth, giving into Paloma's sensual demands, sucking her center until—shaking and gasping— Paloma came against her tongue, and Deanne felt as if her heart had disintegrated into a trillion glittering pieces and poured into Paloma's body in long, pulsating blasts. An illusion, she knew. Paloma already had her heart and always would.

But Paloma felt like heaven.

Like being reborn.

Like…home. Yeah, just like home.

When the intensity waned, Deanne crawled up Paloma's body and lay panting and sweat-sheened above her, hands frozen around the bars above their heads, shaken by the sheer emotional force of their joining. The bedclothes lay rumpled and twined around their ankles, but neither seemed inclined to move. Dee rested her forehead against Paloma's, unmindful of her own tears coursing down Paloma's temples.

They stayed in that position until their chests stopped heaving, until Paloma stirred and moaned. Dee's grip on the bars relaxed and she let her hands slide down and cover Paloma's. All at once Deanne felt it, and her heart jolted. Paloma's ring was back on her finger, where it belonged. Forever. *There is hope.*

Dee raised her face, kissing the moisture from Paloma's cheeks. Paloma stared up, her smile tremulous. Like a flash, Deanne saw them back in high school, steaming her car windows opaque, loving each other with the ferocity and eagerness of pure, raw discovery. A sweet ache filled Deanne, and she said the only words that came to mind, the only appropriate statement for this moment.

"I love you, Paloma Vargas. Forever and a day."

Chapter Seven

From Paloma Vargas's journal, Tuesday, September 25

Holy crap. What was I thinking?

After the languorous, post-orgasmic warmth had cooled in the wee morning hours, reality slammed down on Paloma like a guillotine. *Thwack!* Heck yeah, she'd lost her head. She didn't regret making love with Deanne—far from it. It had been the hottest, most intense sensory and emotional smorgasbord she'd gorged upon in forever, and she'd needed it desperately, especially last night. Every time she flashed back to it, her tummy flopped like a hooked and landed trout. One would think she and Deanne were brand-new lovers, not longtime married folks.

So, no. She didn't regret the lovemaking.

Not a chance.

What she did regret were the complications and assumptions their lovemaking would undoubtedly hurl into the already jumbled mix.

Her stomach jolted. Oh, God. It would be so easy to just give in, to welcome Deanne home and try to block out the unhappiness that'd pushed her to ask for a split in the first place. But that'd be about as effective as a Band-Aid over a stab wound. Facts were facts: as powerful as the passion had been, one night of world-class, gold-medal-winning, come-to-Mama sex still didn't have the strength to erase eight years of growing disillusionment. When the blinding glow of passion had faded, their problems remained, like hulking sentinels in the darkness of reality. She needed Deanne to see that, to accept it, but sincerely doubted she would, considering Paloma's wanton behavior. Heat rose to her cheeks.

Hijole. Talk about sending mixed messages.

She'd told Deanne not to change too much, for fuck's sake! Was she high?

Paloma plucked at the front of her nightgown with nervous fingers, fanning it out to cool her skin. Her dilemma, then, was figuring out how to logically explain her needs. She snatched a coffee mug from the cupboard, filled it. She still wanted Deanne to stay and help with the tight surveillance on Teddy, but that was it. No more sex to confuse the issue—not that she was interested.

Liar.

Okay, if she were completely honest, she *was* interested, despite her better judgment. And she had to admit, though she hadn't believed it to be true, Deanne still seemed fairly attracted to her. Yeah, okay, a lot attracted. A shudder crackled over her flesh like St. Elmo's fire at the memory of *just how much.*

Don't think about it.

She'd even go so far as to say her mind was now open to the possibility of working things out with Deanne. But *working* them out, as in they weren't worked out yet, despite what last night's passion might indicate. Damn. She desperately needed to force the entirety of last night from her brain, heart, nerve endings so she could think clearly, but it was proving a futile pursuit. All the more reason why they couldn't afford to get distracted again by such fiery, all-consuming, mind/body/soul-blitzing sex.

Don't think about it.

She sighed. Why did people always seem to think a rowdy session of stack and wiggle could solve everything from menstrual cramps to estrangement? Not that last night was merely a rowdy session of— *Stop!* Although Paloma heartily wished sex were a magical cure-all, it wasn't. Not this time. But how would she make Deanne see that without seeming as wishy-washy as she felt?

The nagging worry over this impossible tangle of contradictions had kept her wide-eyed and stiff-spined throughout the night as she considered and reconsidered the repercussions. Near dawn, she'd slipped from the warmth of the unexpectedly shared bed, desperate to steal some private moments and reorder her thoughts, organize the facts, and prepare her closing argument. Clarity, distance—she needed them. Common sense, self-restraint— *Good luck, Paloma.*

She shot a glance at the clock and winced. Man, time flew when it was laced with dread. She'd be facing Deanne, the jury of one, any minute now, and she had yet to banish the sensual memory of their tender-fierce lovemaking from her head. Images flashed in her mind's eye like a sultry movie complete with Technicolor and surround sound.

Don't think about it.

Annoyed, she snagged the dishcloth and scoured the already immaculate countertop, simultaneously dreading and listening for Deanne's footsteps in the hall. Fickle, that's what she was.

Girl Most Likely to Waver in Her Decisions.

Girl Least Likely to Stick to Her Guns.

Girl Most Likely to Cave In at the First Sight of Deanne Vargas's Sexy Bedroom Eyes and Toned Abs.

Don't think about it.

No. She clenched her teeth. If she wanted Dee to believe and respect that she'd had enough of being taken for granted, she had to forget last night's pleasurable relapse and let her know exactly where she stood on the issue, the moment Dee entered the room. Just lay it right out—bam!—the world according to Paloma, no questions, no arguments, no hesitation. No wavering. And, no more sex!

No one else will ever be inside you like this.

Paloma sucked in a breath, letting her eyes drift closed. The vigorous scrubbing stilled, her fist clutching the damp cloth as though it was her last tenuous hold on reality. Deanne's sex-whispered words played over and over in her mind. From another woman, they might have sounded ominous, but from Deanne, *her* Deanne, they just sounded…true. And good.

So damn good. God, she wanted Dee again.

No! Don't think about it.

Despite valiant efforts to dam the hot desire, it poured into her limbs like lava. She abandoned the dishcloth, washed and dried her hands, then wrapped her icy fingers around the coffee cup she'd filled. Lifting it until the steam rose to warm her face, she gave herself a mental pep talk.

Buck up, Paloma. You can do this. She took a sip. No matter how delectable Deanne looked or how she'd looked *at her*, Paloma had to somehow make her understand that nothing had been instantaneously solved because of…wow, exactly how many orgasms had they each ended up having? No. No. It didn't matter. She simply must stay in control. More than anything, she absolutely positively *had* to avoid ending up in Deanne's arms, in their bed, beneath her, inside her, again. Or she'd be a goner with a capital "You're So Totally Fucked."

Don't. Think. About. It!

A toilet flushed and a door hinge squeaked in the distance. Her glance jerked toward the hallway, stars spinning into her vision. Clunking the coffee cup down on the water-streaked countertop, she gripped the sink edge, ears perked like a cornered animal's. *Time-out!* She wasn't ready for this. *Okay, wait.* She closed her eyes and ordered herself to take a couple deep breaths. In…out. In… She heard Deanne's voice, then Pep's, and her exhale left her in a whoosh.

Just swell. One would think Pep would be a welcome buffer for this, their first conversation since…that thing Paloma wasn't thinking about…but Pep had his own agenda. She'd have to confront her wife and her little parent trap watchdog all at once, both of them firing their Vargas charm at her with double barrels. *Outnumbered and outgunned.*

Closing her eyes, Paloma crossed herself and pressed a tight kiss to the side of her fist. She'd need more than prayer to resist her woman and her little man, but at least it was a start.

❖

Hot damn. Deanne was a woman with a plan. Finally. And it felt almost as good as that marathon lovemaking session with Paloma last night. Almost. "Go on down to the kitchen, son." She squeezed Pep's small shoulder. "I'm going to check on your brother."

"'Kay!"

Deanne paused with her hand on Teddy's doorknob and watched her older son run down the hallway. Deanne's spirits were unusually high this morning, and—call her cocky—she just had to congratulate herself one more time for her brilliant *winning Paloma back* plan. As she'd lain awake trying to figure out how to keep Paloma beside her in that bed where she belonged, the mother of all brainstorms had struck.

It had required all her self-restraint to fake sleep instead of jumping into action in the middle of the night, but she'd sensed Paloma was awake, too. She couldn't afford to pique her curiosity by leaping from bed and scurrying off through the darkened house.

Deanne allowed a moment to picture Paloma lying next to her, stiff as a board, drawing silent, shallow breaths. She smirked. Punky had never been good at faking sleep. Clearly, she'd been worrying that Dee would try to steamroll her way back into the household after their unexpected lovemaking, which—Paloma would probably be glad to know—wasn't part of the plan. Picturing their mind-altering connection again, Deanne's body quickened.

Don't think about it.

With a grimace, she stretched her neck and shook it off as best she could. No doubt Paloma had rocked her world, and yes, the memories made her hot. But she had to keep her mind out of the bed sheets and on the matter at hand. It was up to Dee to convince Paloma that she planned to let *her* take the lead, so it wouldn't do for her to saunter into the kitchen, aroused and obvious. She stood in the hallway until her desire cooled, then crept into Teddy's room to check him before facing Paloma.

The curtains were drawn, cloaking the room in cool darkness. Teddy slept like a rock, breathing deeply and looking battered but peaceful. Deanne didn't have the heart to wake him, so she settled for tucking the quilt up higher around his little shoulders.

As she tiptoed toward the door, Deanne caught sight of the journal she'd returned to the exact position in which she'd found it last night. A slow smile spread across her face. She hadn't read much of it, just the past few days' worth.

Enough to plant the idea in her subconscious.

Enough to know that Paloma wasn't as dead set on this split as she seemed.

Enough to realize Paloma simply didn't know her way back to the place where they were equal, loving partners and life was damn good.

But as painful as it had been for Deanne to read Paloma's anguished, conflicted words, they helped her realize there was still room to change Paloma's mind, and doing so was Deanne's responsibility. Her resolve strengthened.

At first, she hadn't a clue how to go about it. Lying there imprisoned in insomnia, she'd replayed all the conversations she'd had about or with Paloma since the split. The nonsensical notions had swirled around in her mind like those annoying refrigerator poetry magnets, offering no insight. But finally, the words began to form logical thoughts, and the thoughts eventually led to Deanne's Brilliant Plan.

You forgot me. That's what I can't live with.
Were you attentive?
What about cherish? Did you forget that?
You won her once, Deanne. How did you do it?

Oh, yeah. This had to work. The key to winning Paloma back, Deanne had decided, was written inside her high school journal tucked somewhere in this house. Dee's glimpse inside Paloma's current diary taught her one important fact: Paloma faithfully logged every minute life detail and her feelings about them. So if Dee could find the journals Paloma had kept during their courtship and discover what she'd done right the first time, all she had to do was repeat the steps. Right? If it ain't broke, don't fix it. God, it was inspired. Of course...she didn't know how Paloma would feel when she learned that Dee had read her journals, but...

Definitely don't think about it.

Naturally, Teddy's recuperation was first priority. But while she was living in the house, Deanne also intended to unearth that journal without Paloma suspecting a thing. Before she could search, however, she had to ease Paloma's mind about last night. No pressure—that was her new motto. She was the rookie in this partnership, and the sooner Paloma knew Deanne felt that way, the sooner she'd drop her guard. Principles of combat: Dee wasn't giving up; she was going with the force instead of resisting it.

Not that this was war.

It was love.

But the sooner she located that journal and planned her course of action, the sooner Paloma would be all hers again. Just like last night, only this time it would be forever. Deanne's breath caught.

Don't think about it.

❖

Paloma's heartbeat pounded a reggae steel drum solo by the time a sleep-tousled Pep rounded the corner and sought her out. She expected Deanne to appear at his heels, but Pep was alone. Paloma didn't know whether to be relieved or worried.

"Good morning, beetle bug." She opened her arms, and Pep ran across the tile floor and folded himself against her.

"Hi, Mama."

Her tension eased a notch from the hug. She bent and planted a kiss on the top of his head. "Where's Mommy?"

"Checkin' on Teddy Bedwetty." His eyes raised imploringly. "Do I gotta go to school today?"

"Hmm. We had a pretty scary night." She narrowed her gaze and twisted her mouth to the side as though contemplating it. "I think you can take a mental health day."

"No, but I meant I don't wanna go to school."

She laughed. "That's what a mental health day means."

"Yes!" He extracted himself from her embrace and pumped his arm, boinging around the kitchen like he'd just made the game-winning touchdown. "Can I have Twinkies for breakfast?"

Paloma pinned him with a playful glare. "Quit while you're ahead, Pepito."

He giggled and dragged a kitchen chair to the cereal cupboard, climbing up on it. Before opening the door to peruse his choices, he turned toward her for one more negotiation attempt, wagging his finger. "Okay, cereal. But I get to eat it on the TV tray in the living room and watch cartoons, even though it's not Saturday. Pleeease?"

His teasing persuasion was hard to resist. Why not? He deserved a little reward for his bravery. Besides, having him out of earshot would make it easier for her and Deanne to get over the most awkward part of this unintended morning-after. Ugh!

"All right, but you know the rules. If you spill, I'm gonna have Mommy hang you upside down and clean it with your hair."

Pep gaped, his eyes gleaming. Clearly the idea of becoming a human mop intrigued him. "Nuh-uh!?"

She tickled behind his knee, favoring him with her most playful threatening scowl. "Just don't spill. That'll solve everything."

"'Kay." He opened the cupboard and planted his fists on his hips, eyes searching the multicolored boxes while he made little clicking noises with his cheek. Finally, he pulled out the Cheerios and hugged them to his chest. "What's Teddy gonna eat now that he has jack-o-lantern teeth?"

"Pep, I don't want you teasing your brother, okay? His jaw will be sore and he's probably self-conscious about his missing teeth. Promise me you won't tease. I'm not kidding."

"O-ookay, geez!" Pep rolled his eyes.

She picked up her coffee mug and sipped, considering Pep's question. "I think I'll make him a fruit smoothie. That should go down pretty easily. Would you like one, too?"

Pep retrieved a bowl, then jumped from the chair and fished a spoon out of the drawer. As he headed toward the living room with his spoils, he answered over his shoulder. "Yep, with a strawberry on top. Pretty please, thank you." He shot her a charming grin. "I'll yell when I'm ready."

Another house rule. With permission, the boys could occasionally eat breakfast in front of the television. But either she or Deanne would come pour the milk, and it had to be all gone before the boys could carry their dishes back into the kitchen. Strict, perhaps, but it got them to finish all their milk, and it also saved their carpeting from ruin.

"Not too loud. Teddy's sleeping." She watched him go with a smile on her face, her earlier panic almost completely gone. Pep seemed so carefree this morning, more so than he'd been since... She sighed. Since Deanne had left.

Her anxiety resumed. She still had to face her wife. Setting her coffee aside, she pulled open the refrigerator and bent to ferret through their fruit and yogurt selections. Teddy wasn't as picky as he'd been a few years earlier, thank freaking God. Green leafy vegetables were the enemy, but he'd established a tenuous truce with most fruits.

She had some strawberries and raspberries, a few Clementine oranges, an apple, an Asian pear, and two bananas. She'd have to go to the store later and restock, and made a mental note to pick up pudding and Jell-o and some other soft foods, too. Gathering the fruit and a tub of vanilla yogurt against the front of her nightgown, she straightened carefully and shut the door.

And there stood Deanne.

"Oh!" The fruit tumbled and bounced, rolling in a million different directions across the floor. She managed to keep her grip on the yogurt.

Deanne's eyebrow raised as her eyes tracked the pandemonium. "Well, good morning, Carmen Miranda. I believe you dropped your hat."

Paloma's throat tightened at the sensual rumble of Deanne's voice against her skin, like a rough, promising caress. "Very funny."

Dee bent to retrieve the spilled goods while Paloma just stood there clutching the yogurt to the front of her gown like a twit. What ever happened to staying in control? To keeping the upper hand? Heat swirled over her skin as she watched Deanne stretch and bend. The muscles in her shoulders bunched and flexed, even through the T-shirt. Ugh! She couldn't do this to herself. "I-I'm making a fruit smoothie for Teddy," she blurted.

"Good idea, but it's easiest if you put the fruit in the blender instead of squishing it all over the floor. I mean, I'm just sayin'." Dee stood and loaded everything onto the counter, a thinly veiled smirk on her face.

"Well"—Paloma sniffed haughtily—"you startled me, is all. You can't just sneak up on people."

"Sorry. I'm stealthy like that."

Paloma turned to the sink and began to rinse the fruit under the faucet with jerky, nerve-shot movements. Using peripheral vision, she watched Deanne pull a coffee mug from the cupboard and fill it. Deanne leaned one hip against the counter next to her, and Paloma ceased breathing. Good thing, because Deanne stood too close, and Paloma could still smell the sex on her skin. Way more than her willpower could handle.

"I never meant to scare you, P." The words were a low throaty purr. "Not this morning, and not last night. And on that note, I think we should talk."

Whoa! An involuntary squeeze shot the small green apple she'd been washing straight up into the air. Deanne reached out easily and palmed it, handing it back without a single smart-ass comment. Thank God for small favors. Paloma took it with a shaky hand, barely able to meet Dee's inquisitive eyes. "Yes. We do need to talk, because—"

"Me first," Deanne interjected. "Please."

A sigh breezed from Paloma's lips. What the hell? If the erupting fruit was any indication, she didn't really have her wits about her at the moment anyway. So much for her big assertiveness plans. "Okay. Go ahead."

"Let me get it all out before you say anything." Deanne sipped her coffee, then set the cup aside. "I'm going to jump right in. I don't want us to read too much into what happened, P. That would make things awkward, considering we still have so many issues to deal with. You know?"

Holy— Okay, not what Paloma expected. Stunned. She was stunned. Now she couldn't even blink, much less process her words through her slow-motion brain. Make things awkward? Too many issues?

"Paloma?"

She startled. *Answer!* "Uh, y-yes. I agree."

Dee nodded. "Good." Her voice lowered to a sultry, private purr. "We needed each other last night, and nothing's wrong with that. We're married. We shouldn't feel guilty for, well"—she cleared her throat and smiled almost bashfully—"for, ah…you get my drift, right?"

Forget blinking, she couldn't breathe. Had she heard Deanne right? The woman who didn't want them to feel guilty for making love? Who wasn't going to push the issue?

Who are you, and what have you done with my wife?

"Paloma?" Dee prompted.

"Huh? Oh. Yes. I…I, um, drift. Got it." God, did she ever. Her gaze dropped to Deanne's lips of their own volition and desire swirled in her stomach.

"Anyway, my point." Deanne swiped her palms together. "While Teddy recuperates, I think it'd be best if I slept in the guest room. That way there is no confusion, no added tension. Okay?"

The…guest room? "What did you say?"

Looking cool and calm in direct contrast to her blathering astonishment, Deanne retrieved and sipped her coffee. After swallowing and brushing the back of her hand—God, that hand—over her lips, she added, "I said, I think it would be best if we stuck to our original agreement. Me in the guest room until Teddy is better. You in our bed."

Was it her imagination, or had Deanne's voice sounded like stonewashed velvet when she added the "you in our bed" part? But wait a minute—she was saying exactly what Paloma had planned to tell her. No way! Emie claimed girlfriends/partners/ wives weren't mind readers, but maybe some of them were. Still, Deanne Vargas? Preposterous. Paloma's hand fluttered up to twist her pendant in her fist, a bad nervous habit she needed to break before she broke the chain instead. "But I…thought—"

"You disagree?" Deanne cocked an eyebrow. "That's a surprise. But if you think we should share a bed, I guess—"

"No! No. I just—" She clamped off her words and studied Deanne's face for signs of ulterior motive, but found nothing but sincerity there. This was too good to be true. Maybe there was hope. Paloma released a sigh of tension. "Thank you, Deanne. I worried you'd think…"

"Ah!" Deanne raised a palm and turned her face as if to halt Paloma's words. When she looked back, a slow, sexy smile cut into her cheeks. "No assumptions from here on out." Deanne paused, then headed for the fridge. "Deal?"

Paloma laughed softly and shook her head. "Deal."

This was going to be great, Deanne thought, closing the fridge without removing anything from it. Frankly, she'd needed the full-frontal cold blast before she did something stupid with her flushed, sexily rumpled, but strictly off-limits wife. With zing-zang-boing cartoon sounds carrying in from the living room, Deanne settled against the refrigerator door and watched Paloma wash the fruit. She had seen the tension drain from Paloma once she realized Deanne didn't intend to chain her up as an unwilling—or willing—sexual captive.

An easy smile lifted Deanne's lips, but then Paloma reached for a chopping knife, and the movement drew Deanne's gaze to the smooth skin above the back of her gown. Hungry, feminine appreciation replaced her smile, and her willful mind cast Paloma in the role of that oh-so-willing sexual captive.

Just like that, Deanne was propelled back to last night. Desire ripped through her, and the floor beneath her bucked and undulated. Paloma was so effortlessly beautiful, so guilelessly sexy. Dee wanted her. Wanted to squeeze that orange she was peeling over her chest and lick the tangy juice off her nipples. Deanne might have committed herself to the plan, but she couldn't resist moving up behind and caging Paloma between her arms and the counter.

Paloma's motions stilled, and for a moment Deanne just watched her breath hitch and her hands quiver. Unwilling to push her luck too far, Dee nuzzled through Paloma's tangle of hair until her lips grazed that luscious ear. Paloma's sharp intake of breath seemed to move through her into Deanne, settling low and heavy and hot. "However…just so there's no doubt in your mind…I meant every word I said last night. But all in due time, baby girl. All in due time."

Paloma's lips parted as though she planned to speak, but before she had mustered a response—

"Got milk?" Pep cried out, apparently ready for someone to fix his cereal. Deanne laughed, but Paloma whirled in her arms, eyes searching for escape.

"Let me—I need to—" The telltale hot flush rose on her chest. "I should—"

"I'll get him." Deanne used the front of her body to push off Paloma's, then sauntered lazily away. With calm motions that belied the inner roar, Dee retrieved the milk. Thank God Pep had intervened, Deanne thought with the precious few blood cells that hadn't left her brain for the quick vacation south. Her actions had been just about ready to contradict her promises, which wouldn't do much for the grand plan. Deanne swaggered out of the kitchen, but couldn't resist tossing an innuendo-laden parting shot over her shoulder from the archway. "Hey, I'm glad we talked, Punkybean."

CHAPTER EIGHT

From Paloma Vargas's journal, Monday October 1

I can't believe it's October already, or that a week has passed since Teddy's accident. Thank God he's a resilient little bugger. He's doing great. It's getting harder keeping him still, though, and he can't roughhouse for at least another week. I never thought that boy would grow tired of TV and computer games, but miracles do exist, I've learned.

Speaking of miracles...Deanne, aka the Merry Maid formerly known as my absentee wife. What is up with her? In addition to taking more than her share of turns watch-dogging Teddy every day, she has mysteriously morphed into Ms. Clean. No exaggeration. She's been going like the Energizer Bunny since last Tuesday, and I just can't figure it out. I'm not referring to the regular stuff, like caulking the bathtub or replacing lightbulbs. Deanne has been doing some major cleaning. She not only organized all the closets, scoured the garage, and rearranged the basement, but right now she's up cleaning out the attic, of all things. The attic! It's like the more she digs through fourteen years of accumulated crap, the more she wants to. Freaky. At first I thought she had lost something important, but she said she's just straightening up. Weird. Not that I'm complaining.

It's been so nice having her home. Really home, not like before. I only wish it could be like this all the time, but I know that's a pipe dream. This week's been a false honeymoon.

Blech. Bad choice of words.

Me <———— skeptic.

I want to believe. But, if history is any indication, sooner or later, reality's gonna send me that check. And I'm just not ready.

Standing next to the hanging ladder, Paloma peered up into the sharply angled, wood-beamed attic. Dust motes floated in the wan glow from the portable work light Deanne had carried up, its thick orange cord dangling through the hole like a long lizard's tail. Muffled scratches wafting down from some back corner Paloma couldn't see told her she either had big rats—God forbid—or Deanne was, once again, hard at work. Since rats didn't generally use work lights, Paloma chose to go with option number two. "Dee?"

She winced at the ensuing sounds of items being dropped and Deanne's muffled swear words. Oops. Gray dust rained down on her when Deanne's denim-clad legs moved into her line of sight through the square opening. Paloma backed up and waved her hand in front of her, coughing, then glanced up again, shading her eyes. The closet light succeeded in illuminating the bottom half of Deanne, but her face remained in the shadows. Paloma craned her neck. "I can't see you."

Deanne squatted at the opening, worry lining her dirt-smeared face. "Sorry." She grimaced as more debris tumbled down. "What's up? Teddy okay?"

"He's fine. Restless, though." Paloma brushed a cobweb from her arm, then propped her foot on the bottom rung. "You've been up there forever. How much longer do you think?" Man, did her words have to come out sounding so freaking co-dependent? She hadn't meant it that way at all.

"Oh, uh…"

Deanne shot a glance over her shoulder—at what, Paloma couldn't guess. It had been years since she'd ventured into the attic.

"Let me straighten up. Half an hour or so. You going somewhere?"

"No, but your mom's stopping by, and…" Paloma shrugged, not wanting to admit the terror she felt at the prospect of sitting in that uncomfortable place with Rosario, knowing *everything*. She dreaded thinking of her mother-in-law's probable opinion of their situation. They'd missed the annual Broncos vs. Raiders family football party, and though Teddy's accident had served as the perfect excuse for their absence, Paloma was sure the whole family knew what was up by now. She could just imagine the smoking phone lines between her curious sisters-in-law. The thought of being grist for the Vargas gossip mill turned her stomach.

The familiar war of mixed feelings waged within her heart. Things were so off-kilter. Since they'd made love—a wildly understated term for what they'd *actually* done—she and Deanne had slipped into a warily comfortable routine of living like polite strangers. It wasn't a marriage, but it was better than it had been just before Paloma had asked Deanne to leave. Having her here was comforting, though, and every so often she had an urge to tell Dee to stay. She wasn't sure if she had the strength to disrupt the family again.

But that was settling, wasn't it?

Could she live with herself if she settled?

Then again, could she live with the guilt if she didn't?

"…down in a sec," she heard Deanne say. Her eyelids fluttered as she redirected her attention. "I'm sorry, what?"

"I said, I'll be down in a sec." Deanne cocked her head and frowned with concern. "You okay?"

"Yeah, I'm just…I don't know." Paloma's eyes drifted toward the semidarkness behind Deanne. Though wary of the future, truth was she'd been missing Dee all morning. And ever since Paloma had taken a certain phone message earlier, the deceptively safe cocoon they'd spun seemed on the brink of disintegration. She wanted to hang on.

Unable to think of anything meatier, Paloma cleared her throat and nodded toward the dusty abyss. "Making progress?"

"Well, uh"—unexplained wry humor danced in Deanne's eyes—"not as much as I'd hoped. It's a mess up here."

"So I see. Find any treasures amongst cobwebs?"

A rather sick little smile curved Dee's lips. "Not yet, but I haven't given up hope." She clapped her palms together, sending another warren of dust bunnies hopping. "Well, the sooner I can get through this, the sooner I'll be down."

"Okay. Um…" Paloma ran her fingers through her hair and stared at the wall, thinking of the phone call. Now or never. It wasn't fair or reasonable to hide it. She couldn't keep reality at bay forever, and wasn't reality the true litmus test of whether or not she and Deanne would survive this, anyway?

Tilting her head back, she met Deanne's gaze directly. "Nora Obermeyer called. She said she was returning your call."

Realization flickered then faded in Deanne's eyes. "Oh, good."

Paloma waited for Dee to elaborate. Naturally, she didn't. Instead, she averted her gaze. "I'll call her when I'm done. Thanks."

That old, familiar bitterness surged. So Deanne wasn't gonna tell her squat, was that it? She should've known. *Let it drop, Paloma.* She really should. The woman had responsibilities, after all. But why the furtiveness? Why couldn't they discuss things like a couple? She huffed. Just another barb-edged reminder that they still *weren't* back to being a couple in some ways that really counted.

That all-too-familiar pain of abandonment clouded Paloma's

common sense. She didn't even try to keep the wounded tone from her cutting words. "Itching to get back to work, now that you're stuck here with me and the boys?"

"It's not that, P." Deanne sounded defeated, as if she'd both expected—and dreaded—this very reaction from Paloma.

The fact that she was so predictable bothered Paloma. "What, then?"

Deanne studied Paloma, lines of worry bracketing her mouth. "Listen to yourself. It's all there."

She frowned, confused. "What is?"

"Doubt. Resentment. Anger. Bottom line is, things will never heal between us until you trust that I can be less of a...a workaholic. My word means nothing to you"—she held up a hand when Paloma opened her mouth to protest—"and I understand that. I do. But I can't regain your trust until I go back to work and prove myself, P, so why prolong the agony, to use your words."

Paloma set her jaw. Jackass! Deanne had a point. Paloma didn't want her to have a point, especially not in this case, because it made Paloma come off as a total shrew. She really wanted to be the reasonable adult in all this—start to finish. Not as the snippy, bitter wife.

And she was doing so well.

Not.

"We've made progress, Paloma, but nothing's settled. We both need to know where we're headed." Deanne paused, the silence yawning between them. Her earnest look dared Paloma to deny it. "Am I right?"

Paloma wrapped her arm through the rungs and leaned her face against the ladder. At least Deanne had admitted she was a workaholic. That was something. "I guess." Paloma couldn't help but fear that their tentative connection would unravel the minute Deanne donned that uniform and returned to her first love—the job. The thought of being hurt again terrified Paloma. An immature part of her wanted to lash out now just to protect her heart from the inevitable pain.

"I have to work, P." Deanne's voice was a patient purr. "We need money to live."

"I know," she said, on a wave of guilt. Damn. If she wanted Dee to communicate with her, she should extend the same courtesy. Checking the attitude in her voice, she sighed. "I'm sorry. It's just, things are improving, like you said. I worry you'll revert—"

"Paloma," Dee interrupted, her tone laced with gentle skepticism. "This week's been nice, yes. But you have to admit, it hasn't been a marriage." She spread her arms. "We're not even sleeping together. Is that how you want forever to look?"

Paloma's stomach cramped. "I…want to work things out. I'm just scared."

"I know you are. Still, I can't just be your roommate. I want to be your partner, and…God, I want to be your lover. But not until you accept me completely." A pause. "That won't happen until you're no longer scared. Until you trust me. And none of *that* will happen until I go back to work. You've got to give me a fighting chance."

Paloma chewed the inside of her cheek, grudgingly admiring Deanne's thoughtfulness about the topic, her effort. Offering an olive branch of sorts, Paloma said, "You sound pretty convinced that you can."

"I am." Her expression segued from frustration to guarded playfulness with a single wink. "Now I just have to convince you."

Hope bubbles floated inside her, but—*pop! pop! pop!*— disappeared just as quickly. The path of least resistance would be sucking it up and letting Deanne stay. The easiest path, however, often led to the deepest dissatisfaction, and Paloma couldn't bear to settle for less than she deserved any longer. Not with Deanne. She was trying—Paloma would give her that. But did Dee have it in her to change for the long haul? She supposed Deanne was right—she would never know unless she let go.

So, fine.

She would.

But fear made her lift her chin and drill Deanne with a stare. "Whether you go back right away or not, I can't make you any promises."

"I'm not asking for promises. All I want is a chance." Deanne stilled then, waiting for Paloma's acquiescence. When she remained silent, Deanne added, "You and the boys are the most important part of my life, but work is a part of it, too. I won't let it get in the way again, but I have to put at least some of my energy there." Deanne sat on the edge of the attic entryway and reached her hand down.

After a moment of staring at it, remembering it touching her body, admiring the subtle shine of the worn wedding band against Deanne's brown skin, Paloma stepped up a rung and slid their palms together. Deanne rubbed her knuckles with a thumb and smiled.

Paloma's heart beat so hard, she couldn't do more than stare back.

"I love you so fucking much, P, and I don't want to settle any more than you do. If you find you can't trust me one hundred percent, can't believe in me—" Deanne pressed her lips together for a moment, unable or unwilling to complete the thought. "Please try, baby girl."

"I am trying. It's not that easy."

Deanne squeezed her fingers gently. "I'm not asking for favors. I need you to trust me because you *do*, not just because I want you to."

Damn. Did Paloma dare believe? She ached to, with every fiber of her soul. In a moment of weakness, she blurted, "You know, you don't have to leave again." She cleared her throat, feeling faint. "We can…figure something out."

"No, babe," Deanne whispered. "I can't stay. Not until you can welcome me back as your partner. You ready for that?"

Paloma's silence was a clear answer.

The corner of Deanne's lip twitched. "When you're ready, not before. Ruben doesn't mind me staying there."

Paloma swallowed thickly. "But the boys need you here."

Pain pulsed like lightning over Deanne's expression. "The boys." After a long pause, she blew out a controlled breath. "Fine. I'll stay for the boys. In the guest room. But things have to change between us if I'm going to stay for the long run. I can't bear to play the roommate. And I can't bear to see resignation in your eyes every time I look at you."

"I know," Paloma said, softly.

"Which is why I have to go back to work."

She sagged, accepting it. Deanne was right. "Okay."

One of Deanne's eyebrows quirked. "Okay?"

Jesus. One little brow waggle and Paloma wanted to make love to her. Right here, right now. Dust bunnies and dirt be damned. She yearned for Deanne to convince her she really, truly meant what she said. She was warm and lean, feminine and... Deanne. So beautiful. Fearful of her own weakness, Paloma tried for a haughty tone. "What part of 'okay' don't you understand?"

Deanne laughed softly, gazing at her with so much love it stole her breath. Soon Dee's expression darkened into something earthier, full of promise. Paloma thought Dee might pull her up and kiss her, but the peal of the doorbell tore through the tenuous electricity crackling between them.

Paloma snatched her hand away, anxiety flooding her. "Oh no, that's your mother."

Deanne shook her head as if Paloma had gone crazy. "It's my *mom*, not the grim reaper. She loves you, remember?"

"Maybe she did, but now?" *Ding-dong.* Paloma looked at the doorway, sick and terrified. "You did tell her, right?"

"You know I did. Stop worrying."

"But what exactly did she say when—?"

"Paloma, I already told you. She—"

"Mama!" hollered Teddy, from the living room.

"Shoot. I don't want Teddy riled up. Just hurry, please?"

"Hey. It'll be fine. We're family. We've been family for a long time, and that hasn't changed."

Paloma didn't respond. Couldn't. But, God, how she yearned for those words to be true.

❖

Paloma had managed small talk, coffee, and more than her fair share of nervous gestures since greeting Rosario in the foyer. Now, if she could just shake this complete intimidation…

She glared daggers at the ceiling. Where the hell was Deanne?

She'd left Rosario in the living room to baby Teddy like only an *abuelita* could, grateful for the space and time to catch her breath, but it passed all too quickly. She peered up as Rosario bustled through the archway and smiled across the cut-away kitchen counter. The thermal coffee carafe and thick mugs were on the table, and Paloma was almost done slicing the banana bread Emie'd brought over the day before. She managed an overbright excuse for a smile.

"Have a seat. The coffee's fresh." God. She felt so falsely cheery, like some pinafore-wearing super-wife wannabe from a blighted episode of a 1950s sitcom. Her inane words came in a rapid-fire tumble she didn't seem able to control. "Deanne will be down in a sec. She's been cleaning, well, everything. The basement, the closets, now the, uh, the attic. I can't figure it out"—she blurted a dumb little laugh, her movements flighty as a hummingbird. Desperation treated her to a virtual lobotomy— lovely.

Help, I'm talking and I can't shut up!

"Anyway, Emie brought this bread, which goes really well with the coconut coffee. She makes great banana bread. I need to get the recipe, I keep telling myself. Give me a minute, I'll—oh, I have butter. Do you care for some jam, too?"

"Ah, *m'ija.*" Rosario's lined, bronze face warmed with compassion and...regret? She turned a chair from the table to face the kitchen and sank into it, smoothing the skirt of her plaid cotton shirtwaist. "Don't be so nervous around me, honey. I've known you since you were a girl, and there's no judgment here. Marriages have problems." She pursed her lips. "I know Deanne or any of my boys aren't the easiest people to live with."

Yikes, straight to the bone. Paloma sighed. What could she say? *You're right? Your daughter's a pain in my ass, but I love her anyway?* "I'm sorry. I don't mean to..."

"They had a hard time with their father being gone." Rosario's attention was focused on some distant memory that faded the normally bright light in her eyes like a day-old corsage. "I tried my best, but—" She shrugged, letting the half-statement stand.

Paloma felt a kick in the chest that nearly knocked her backwards. God, Rosario worked three jobs supporting those kids. She shouldn't shoulder any blame. "Rosi, you did a wonderful job raising them. None of this is your fault."

"Nonsense. I'm Deanne's mother." One black eyebrow arched. "You're saying she got all her traits from Victor's side? You wanna put me in an early grave?"

"Of course not, but Deanne's a grown woman." Paloma stacked the banana bread on a plate with shaking hands and pulled two butter knives from the drawer. "She makes her own decisions."

"That doesn't keep me from feeling badly that there are problems, or from praying that you and Deannita work through them and stay together, *amada.* She needs you."

Ugh. Guilt trip, boarding here. Watch your step and carry your own baggage.

"Well, we need her, too. But—"

"You need all of her, no?"

"Y-yes." Paloma sighed. "And I haven't had all of Deanne since—"

"The boys were born," Rosario finished.

Surprise zinged through Paloma. "How did you—?"

"I understand more than you think." Rosario shook her tiny, veined fist. "I'm her mother, but I'm also a woman, just like the two of you."

Paloma's heart swelled with humble gratitude. She should've known Deanne's mother would be reasonable. Rosario knew Deanne better than anyone, save Paloma herself. "I don't want to speak badly about your daughter, though. I respect you too much for that."

"Talking it out isn't the same as talking badly." Rosario sighed. "I make no claims that my kids are perfect."

Paloma chewed her lip. "Well, one problem, the woman's got a one-track mind: work. It doesn't leave a whole lot of room for me and my needs."

The older woman clucked her tongue. "Ay, that girl. She wants to give of herself, Paloma. She just tries too hard sometimes and doesn't stop to figure out what other people need instead of what she *thinks* they need. She's always been that way. Gets it from Victor's side," Rosi added with disgust. "And now, with Pep and Teodoro. I'm sure Deanne's trying to be a better parent than Victor was."

Paloma frowned. "Of course she's a better parent than Victor. How could she even think otherwise?"

Rosario gave an enigmatic shrug. "Who knows what goes on in someone's head, in someone's heart?"

Paloma carried the bread to Rosario, then sat and plunked her elbows on the table and supported her chin with her palms. "Wives are so annoying. Especially Vargas wives."

Rosario laughed and stirred some thick, white *crema* into her coffee. "I know that more than most, *hija*. Goes for Vargas husbands, too. I married and divorced one and raised four more plus Deanne. But my girl—that one's got a good heart. She's terrified to lose you and the boys. That's why she spins her wheels so much."

Paloma chewed her bottom lip, fighting not to cave in under

the weight of her respect for this wise, wise woman. "Spinning her wheels is what's pushing me away. I want to work things out. I do. But I can't just forgive Deanne all her faults, write them off as remnants of her childhood, and endure anymore."

"*Claro*. I'm not suggesting you stay if you're unhappy." Rosario's clear, dark eyes danced away. She toyed with her napkin. "I just hoped to help you understand Deanne better, so maybe you could find compassion."

"We all have issues from childhood, mine being the fact that I was raised to make my bed and lie in it. But I don't want an old-fashioned marriage, Rosi. No offense to your generation of women." Paloma sighed with frustration. "We have to choose to change patterns from childhood if they aren't working anymore."

"Oy-yoy-yoy...this I know, honey." Rosi sipped.

"Deanne needs to compromise. That's all I'm saying." Paloma twisted her mouth, pleading for understanding. "I need her completely or not at all. Because it hurts too much otherwise."

"*Sí*." Rosario leaned forward and covered Paloma's hand with her own. "Find a chance for Deannita in your heart, *m'ija*. It's not fair of me to ask that, but I love you both, and the boys." She shrugged an apology. "Frankly, I'm getting to old to care about convention or fairness. I just want my children happy, and Deanne"—she laughed dryly—"that one needs you to be happy, Paloma. Trust me—a mother knows."

Paloma smiled, realizing finally that she had an ally in Rosario, not a foe. "I'm trying."

"Don't misunderstand me, little one. I'm not telling you to compromise your needs. I just pray you and Deanne don't give up too soon. For the boys as much as for yourselves."

Paloma's throat ached, and she glanced away, picking at the crust of the banana bread for which she had no appetite. "I'm... not giving up. I still love her, Rosi—"

"*¡Bueno!* That's all I need to know," Rosario spread her palms out flat to signal the end of the explanations. She wore a smug cat-who-ate-the-canary look. "The rest is God's will and your business." She nodded with finality. "Now. How about some of that bread, hmm?"

❖

Freaking Jackpot.

Given her limited time, Deanne had launched into the final few minutes of journal hunting with the fervor of a gambling addict on her last roll of quarters. Luckily, it had paid off. *Ka-ching!* She stared down at the box marked journals with excitement building in her chest. She no longer cared about the cobwebs clinging to her skin, her sore muscles, or the dust coating her lungs. She'd found them, at last.

Naturally, she'd found them in the very last place she looked, because Murphy was a bitch and she had laws. Had she started this hunt in the attic, she wouldn't have had to suffer through cleaning all those closets. Or the damn garage. Not to mention the basement.

But it didn't matter, because here they were, and as a bonus, Paloma thought she was some kind of broom-toting knight in shining armor for decluttering the house. Teddy was on the mend, life was calming down, and soon Deanne would have the answers she needed to win Paloma back.

She snapped open the blade of her Spyderco knife, kneeling carefully to slit the sealing tape. Hooking the knife back onto her belt, she lifted the cover, which stirred up another dust devil. Turning her head, she sneezed twice, then her watering eyes sought the prize. The priceless book of answers. The jour—

Oh no. Deanne's excitement fizzled like a birthday candle dropped in the bathtub. Journal, her ass. There had to be a hundred journals in this box. Why'd Paloma have to be so damned prolific? Blowing out a frustrated sigh, Deanne looked toward the corner of the attic, rubbing her knuckles across the edge of her jawline thoughtfully.

What now, Einstein?

No way could she stay up here long enough to find the one she needed. Hell, she didn't even *know* which one she needed. Mom had been here more than half an hour, and Paloma was no doubt fuming because she hadn't shown her face. The last thing she wanted was to disappoint Paloma *again*. Pissing her off probably wasn't the best way to launch the grand plan. Not to mention, Deanne felt certain Paloma's curiosity—or annoyance—would eventually send her up that drop-ladder into the attic. The thought of getting busted before she even began settled on Deanne's shoulders.

Replacing the cover, Deanne camouflaged the box and started down the ladder toward the sound of Paloma's and Mom's voices in the kitchen. This unexpected obstacle rankled, but she tried to stave off the annoyance. Just a minor setback.

She'd have to resort to plan B…Emie and Iris.

They were Paloma's best friends. Surely they'd remember which journal Paloma had used that particular year in high school. Granted, Deanne hadn't wanted to involve anyone else, but she needed a hand. The trick would be convincing Emie and Iris to help…*and* to keep the secret from Paloma.

Deanne arrived at Common Grounds coffee shop early, grateful she'd been able to get away from the house. Relief had flowed through her when she'd entered the kitchen to find Paloma and Mom chatting away like always. She offered to grocery shop while they visited, and—thank God—she'd reached Emie and Iris, who agreed to meet her right away.

Lenny Kravitz crooned in the background of the brick-walled coffee shop, and the smell of freshly ground Jamaican beans and pungent spices hung in the air. Two dapper white-haired gentlemen played checkers by the front window. A woman tapped away on her laptop against the wall. A young couple sat losing themselves in each other's eyes at the round-top nearest the bookshelves.

Deanne ordered a house coffee—black—and waited by the counter until the barista, a multi-pierced young man wearing a hemp shirt, baggy jeans, and Chakra wristbands, was done serving other customers.

One of his bejeweled eyebrows rose. "Did I forget something?" His hands worked with practiced efficiency over the coffee maker's many gleaming parts.

"No, just a request." Deanne held her palm up to indicate "so-high." "I'm looking for two women. A petite pregnant lady and one who looks like a supermodel."

The barista smirked, squinting as steam rose in his face. "I can respect your dream, brah, but this is a coffee shop, not Fantasy Island."

Deanne barked a laugh. "No, these are actual women. I guess I should've said, I'm *expecting* them." Deanne jerked a thumb over her shoulder. "When they get here, do you mind telling them I'm in the back?"

"Sure thing. A pregnant lady and a supermodel," he mumbled wryly, finishing off a macchiato with a flourish of cream. "That'll be hard to miss."

A few minutes later, Emie and Iris entered the back room, each holding a thick ceramic mug.

"What's with that guy up front?" Iris asked, mystified. "We walked in and I swear he laughed out loud at us."

"Probably caffeine overdose." Deanne stood, taking their cups while they removed jackets and settled in. "Thanks for meeting me. I'm sorry I called at the last minute."

"No problem." Emie smiled. "How's Teddy?"

"Bouncing back like a boomerang." They'd been lucky on that count.

"Kids are so hardy. *Pobrecito.*" Iris tossed her hair and then rested her elbows on the table. "So, what's urgent, Deanne V.?"

Iris, Dee realized, would be the harder sell. She was super-protective of Paloma. "I need information." Deanne's heart pounded.

Iris looked skeptical.

"Tell us." Emie interlaced her fingers over her belly.

Deanne looked from one to the other. "Do you know when Paloma fell in love with me?"

A confusion-thickened pause ensued.

"Um…D? Honey?" Iris said, as though Deanne was several colors short of a full 96-count crayon box. "We all went to school together, if you'll recall. Dumbass. Of course we know."

Deanne shook her head. "No, I mean, exactly *when* did she fall in love with me? The time period. I need to know."

"Oh. Tenth grade," Iris told her, just as Emie said, "Definitely junior year."

Iris peered quizzically at her. "What are you talking about, Em? You think it wasn't until junior year? They were together most of tenth."

Emie wagged her index finger. "Yeah, but then Paloma's dad made them break up for the summer before eleventh because of the 'getting too serious' thing, remember?"

Deanne groaned. "I sure as hell remember."

Emie smiled, then continued her explanation to Iris as though Deanne wasn't there. "That summer apart was what sealed it for Pea. They hadn't reached point of sale until after that, remember? Pea was still unsure. Junior year, Deanne morphed into Ms. Perfect—"

"Yes, then." Deanne leaned forward, a spark of hope flaring inside her. Two pairs of eyes met hers. "That's what I want. The year I was…uh—"

"Ms. Perfect? Eleventh grade." Emie nodded, certain.

"Now that I think about it, Em is right."

Deanne cleared her throat. "You don't happen to remember what journal Paloma used then, do you?"

"Ugly neon swirl." In stereo. The women smiled at each other. "Spiral bound," Iris added, sipping her coffee.

"It had lyrics to Cyndi Lauper's 'Girls Just Wanna Have Fun' on the cover," Emie added.

Iris choked her coffee down and laughed through the resulting cough. "Oh my God, I hated that cover. It was so…*Tiger Beat*."

All three laughed, but Deanne sobered quickly.

"So, what's with these cryptic questions?" Emie asked.

This was it. Now or never. "I need to read it."

Iris balked. "What? You can't, D. That's an invasion of privacy. And you're a *cop*!"

"Well, in the Colorado statutes—"

"Drop the cop garble." Iris clicked her tongue. "What would your mother say?"

"She'd say 'get your wife back. Whatever it takes.' It's not illegal."

Iris sat straighter. "Yeah, but morally—"

"Hang on." Deanne held up her hands. "Just listen. I don't make a habit of reading Paloma's journals"—she felt a small stab of guilt at the just-left-of-true statement—"but I'm fucking desperate. My marriage is in trouble. I won't sit idly by and watch it end." She splayed both palms on her chest. "I'll take full responsibility—"

"Damn right you will," Iris said.

"What's the journal's connection with your relationship problems anyway?" Emie looked intrigued.

Their wary expressions told Deanne she hadn't fully explained her intent yet. She didn't even know if she could. She wasn't as good at this girl stuff as Paloma and her best friends. She covered Emie's left hand, Iris's right, with her own. "Look, I wouldn't even consider reading it if I thought there was any other way."

"To what?" Iris shot her a narrowed scowl.

"To win her back." Paloma's two best friends stared at her as though she'd asked them to run a hit.

"Huh?" Iris looked baffled and dubious all at once. "With a sixteen-year-old journal? Oooo—kayyy."

"What exactly do you intend to do?" Emie asked.

Deanne grabbed her coffee cup, turning it around and around between her fingers. "See, I don't want her to take me back because she feels obligated or just gives in. I need to show her she can trust me. That I'm worthy of her love."

Iris leaned in and snapped her fingers twice. "Deanne, you're a woman. Speak chick. You aren't making a bit of sense."

"Okay, Jesus, give me a chance. Man, you two are a rough audience." Deanne cleared her throat. "I'm hoping that particular journal will tell me what I did right the first time." She pressed her lips together. "It's a long shot, I know. But I'm going to win her back by…doing whatever I did to make her fall in love with me in high school. Again."

There, she'd said it. The room hung in suspended animation. Both women stared, open-mouthed. Then, as though a magic romance fairy had sprinkled her beguiling dust over them, their surprised expressions softened into something downright dreamy. "Awwwwww," they sighed, before exchanging one of their über-chick looks that had always made Deanne nervous.

"DV, you big romantic fool." Iris sighed. She punched Deanne in the arm, but her face showed approval. "You're going to recreate your courtship?"

Huh. Deanne hadn't imagined she could sum up her brilliant plan in so few words, but there it was. "In a nutshell, yes."

Iris clicked her tongue. "You really do love her, in your own infuriating way, don't you? That's so sweet."

"I love her more than life itself."

"Just don't resort to that Flock of Seagulls hairdo you tried. That was an epic fail." Iris smirked.

"Okay, read the Cyndi Lauper journal." Emie's expression was warm. "But if Paloma finds out and flips, you're on your own."

"Absolutely." Deanne hung her head. When she'd recovered from the acute flush of relief, she looked up. "Thanks for understanding."

Emie patted her hand, and Iris said, "You never quite know what you have until you lose it, huh, Deanne?"

"Not true. I always knew." She quirked her mouth to the side. "I guess I just didn't know how to show it."

CHAPTER NINE

From Paloma Perea's neon-swirl, Cyndi Lauper journal, end of September, 11th grade

> *Oh my God, I think Deanne Vargas is going to ask me to homecoming!!!!! I totally didn't know if we'd get back together this year after the split. Man! I get pissed every time I think about Daddy making me and Deanne break up for the summer because he thought we were "getting too serious." Jump back—we haven't even been to third base! It sucked totally!!*
>
> *I heard Deanne went out with Renee Montoya over the summer, and I was depressed to the max. I played my soundtrack from Endless Love over and over, crying and missing her. I hate thinking there was ANY other girl, but I'd rather it be anybody other than skanky Renee. If her bangs get any taller, her head will need its own zip code. Gag me!!!*
>
> *Anyway, Deanne's, like, the baddest chick in the whole school, and I want to go to homecoming with her! No—I want to marry her!! Wait—lesbians can't really get married, right? Well, who cares. WE would be married. Wouldn't we have the cutest little daughters?*
>
> *Paloma Vargas.*

That sounds awesome.

Paloma + Deanne 4ever

I've been stressed since school started that Deanne found someone new. Iris says I shouldn't worry. I'd die if Dee took someone else, though. Noelle Ruiz (witch) said she'd heard Deanne was asking Renee (skank). So, I'm not for sure she's gonna ask me. But Kathy Pirelli overheard Jenna Gaston talking to Deanne's friend, Reyna What's-her-face—that other track jock—and Kathy said Jenna told her she heard something like Deanne was going to have Reyna ask me tomorrow at lunch. Totally rad!

Anyway, I think Deanne will ask. She sent ME a carnation on sweetheart's day. The frosh delivered them during third hour, which was bitchin' since Noelle (witch) is in my class. She was, like, totally ragged off about it. She kept staring hard at me through those spidery stiff eyelashes. I'm sorry, I don't like that chick. She's, like, the total biggest home wrecker in our class.

One other cool thing. Emie said Deanne was totally scoping me out before sixth yesterday. I knew she was standing there with Reyna, so I kind of played like I didn't see them so Deanne wouldn't think I was a dweeb. It's so hard not knowing what she feels. I should be totally assertive and have one of my friends ask her if she wants to get back together, but it would bite if she said no, and then I'd look like a TOTAL freak. I guess I'll just wait and see if Reyna asks me to go to the dance with Deanne. Then, I'll know once and for all.

I'm in love!!!!

If Mama and Daddy don't let me go, I'll sneak out, swear to God. This is MY LIFE, and, I mean, GOD, I'm 16 years old. When are they going to start treating me like an adult??? It's so tedious!

Anyway, I'm so spazzed! I'm going to starve next

week so I can lose five pounds before the dance. I want a red dress, too. This month's Glamour said red is the new black, whatever that means. Daddy will probably have a cow. Ugh!

I have to study, but I totally hope Deanne asks me!!! Getting asked to homecoming is practically like getting an engagement ring!!! I'd know for sure she still liked me then. Everyone would. Totally awesome!

Deanne set the journal on the center console of the patrol car and glanced around the deserted lot where she'd parked against the closed factory building. The radio had been quiet. She usually spent downtime stopping cars and contacting suspicious people, but she'd been back at work for nearly a week, and this was the first chance she'd had to dig into the journal. Plus, work was the only place she *knew* Paloma wouldn't bust her.

Deanne snapped off her red shoulder lamp, dousing the interior of the cruiser in darkness, and then just sat there with her head buzzing. Teens were so...*weird.* Of course, she liked knowing Paloma had considered her the "baddest chick in the whole school." A cocky grin lit her face. Paloma had puppy-loved her, even back then. What a feeling.

But P's teenage angst was exhausting to read. Amusing, too. Deanne didn't remember them being quite so...well, *teenaged.* Paloma dotted every "i" and "j" with a little heart. Seriously. A puffy little heart.

Nobody escaped that gawky stage, she supposed.

Odd how the years, a mortgage, and a few kids could alter a person's perspective.

Deanne could, however, relate to Paloma's constant "she loves me, she loves me not" agony over their budding relationship. She'd felt just as needy and unsure about her, especially during that interminable summer apart before junior year. Her gut swirled with the awful memory. At age seventeen, panting with hormones, three months without Paloma Perea had been Deanne's private version of hell. But their love had endured then, and it would again.

Deanne fingered the neon cover, shaking her head. Had Paloma really thought Deanne would've chosen another girl over her? And Renee, of all people?

Everyone knew she was a skank.

Dee barked a laugh, followed by a tired groan. She was seriously losing her luggage on this surreal trip down memory lane.

The truth was, she'd spent that whole miserable summer hanging with her track buddies, trying not to look like the lovesick pup she was. But now she understood Mr. Perea's concern. Beyond the whole gay thing, the man had probably taken one look at Deanne's face and feared for his daughter's virtue. Rightly so. At seventeen, it'd been physiologically impossible to keep her brain out of Paloma's pants. She'd wanted Mr. Perea's little girl something bad.

Still did…

Deanne shook the enticing thoughts from her brain. Enough reminiscing. What had she learned from the journal that would help her win Paloma back? First, young Paloma had yearned for confirmation that she was *Deanne's girl*. That need probably hadn't changed much. Also, she used to think an invitation to homecoming was akin to an engagement—

Whoa. Deanne went completely still. Brainstorm.

Big brainstorm.

She checked her Ironman watch and drummed her fingers on the steering wheel, a wholeheartedly cheesy plot formulating in her head. Oh, yeah. This idea was made-for-TV corny, but that lent it an odd charm. Did she dare? Deanne's embarrassed laughter rang loudly in the patrol car.

If the dreamy expressions on Emie's and Iris's faces at the coffee shop had been any indication, Paloma might be able to appreciate this ridiculous gesture, purely for its sappy intent.

It could work if Deanne didn't take it too seriously, and really, how could she? Plus, Paloma was worth every ounce of potential humiliation she'd feel if this didn't work.

But it would. It could.

It just so happened that her old pal, Reyna Falcon, was the high school track coach now, and coincidentally, homecoming was two weekends away. Divine providence…

Snatching up her cell phone, Deanne dialed information for Reyna's number. She'd bet, for the promise of a hosted and catered pay-per-view sports night, she could bribe Reyna into asking Paloma if she'd go out with "the baddest chick in the school" again. Just for old time's sake. Reyna had always been a good sport, the first to jump all over a dare. What the hell? Deanne had everything to gain—Paloma and their life together—and nothing to lose except her dignity.

Definitely dice Deanne was willing to roll.

Almost two weeks back at work, and Deanne was living up to her promises. Paloma had to give her points for that. Dee had taken an afternoon of sick time to accompany her and Teddy to the doctor. She got the boys dressed and fed on the mornings Paloma had yoga class. She asked about Paloma's day, brought tea to her room every night, chose home life instead of overtime. Deanne had even helped her pick out her very first college classes.

Paloma could slowly, surely, feel trust for the woman she loved seeping back into her soul. If she weren't ten times bitten, a hundred times shy, she might have to admit that, yes, the wake-up call she'd given Deanne had actually worked.

Even though, Dee had been acting so…odd lately.

Not only had she begun playing albums from their high school years, but there were the flowers. On Monday, the daisy was on Paloma's nightstand with a note from Deanne saying how much she loved her. Tuesday, blue bachelor's buttons had been in the bathroom sink. The note spoke of trust and commitment and second chances. Wednesday's green carnation and Thursday's yellow tulip? The shower and the kitchen counter, respectively. One note about Pep, the second about Teddy. Today's blood red rose had rested atop the pillow on Deanne's side of the bed, and the note—

Phew, that note.

Paloma's face flamed. Let's just say she'd keep that particular missive aside for her own private pleasure, thank you very much.

But, yeah. Something was definitely up with Deanne.

Paloma was discussing just that with Iris and Emie that Friday morning, when they'd gotten together to browse the attendants' wear catalogs Iris had checked out from the lesbian wedding planner's office. The three friends stood by the dinette and stared at the vase of flowers. Paloma had arranged them on the table with the closed notes for her friends' examination. Deanne had even folded the letters in that silly, tucked-corner way they used back in junior high.

"See?" Her sweeping gesture took in the whole display. "Isn't it freaky?"

Iris picked up a neatly folded note and turned it over in her hand. "I don't even remember how to fold stuff like this anymore," she mused. "But you used to live to get these from Deanne."

"Uh, yeah. A zillion years ago when we were young and stupid."

"So? Don't be so stuffy and grown-up, sheesh. It's sweet," Emie said. "You don't have to be a teenager to appreciate sweet."

Paloma quirked her mouth. They weren't getting her point. Maybe this would help. She planted her hands on her hips. "You know what was playing on the stereo when I woke up today? 'Stairway to freakin' Heaven.'"

"Oh, isn't that the first slow song you and Deanne danced to? That's perfect!" Emie exclaimed, clapping.

"Good song, but it got really fast at the end, remember?" Iris crinkled her nose. "You never knew whether to dance all jerky and fast or just say 'thanks for the twirl' and split. Not the easiest slow-dance song, if I remember correctly."

Paloma couldn't help but chuckle. Okay, so the nostalgic music was rather charming. But strange, too. "Listen to me, you guys, I'm serious. The day before, I ate breakfast to strains of 'Always and Forever,' and last Monday before bed, the woman actually played Rick James's 'Super Freak.'"

Iris muffled a laugh against the side of her fist.

"Paloma, it's cute," Emie assured her. "Why so worried?"

She treated them to a good-natured glare. "I'm beginning to think Deanne smacked her head instead of Teddy."

Iris and Emie exchanged a smile.

"If you want my opinion, I think it's romantic and you're overreacting," Iris said.

"I agree." Emie grinned.

"Traitors." Paloma pulled a face. "You're no help."

Iris patted her hand. "What's wrong with a little romance, Pea?"

"Nothing. I don't know." She crossed her arms. "I suspect she's trying to butter me up."

Iris rolled her hand. "And the problem with that is?"

"I don't"—she sighed—"if you must know, it's kind of working."

"Aha!" Emie smirked. "Just enjoy the attention, Paloma. Romantic gestures aren't meant to be analyzed to death."

Iris flicked her hand over and studied her nails with nonchalance. "How's it going since Deanne went back to work?"

Paloma's heart fluttered with an unfamiliar feeling of hope and anticipation. "Great so far. It's been exactly how I always knew

it could be. But…it's lulling me into a feeling of false security."
Heat prickled over her skin, followed closely by chagrin. "I'm
starting to forget how bad things had gotten and focus on whether
or not it would be wise to jump her bones."

"Do it!" Emie urged.

Paloma bit her lip. She wanted to. So much. If only Deanne
had acted this wonderful from the get-go. "What if it's the calm
before the storm?"

Iris rolled her eyes. "Damn, Pea. Have you ever stopped to
consider that maybe the storm already ripped up your coast and
moved on? This might just be the clean-up part, you know, like
after a hurricane." She reached out to touch the red rose. "Think
of these flowers as Red Cross volunteers who've come to patch
things up and rebuild docks."

Paloma and Emie started laughing. "Oh my God, Iris is
waxing poetic. We need to get to that commitment ceremony, and
soon." Paloma snapped her fingers softly and held out her hand.
"Enough. Give me those catalogs." They'd hemmed and hawed,
then decided on dresses. Simple dresses, and nothing in baby-shit
brown. "We have to make sure you don't costume us like bright
little crumpets for the ceremony."

"Oh, but check this out." Iris opened a catalog to the picture
of a very brief, very tight fuchsia gown with wide holes running
up both sides. She sucked in her cheeks. "Better crumpets than
strumpets, my pals."

The old friends erupted into laughter again, just as the
doorbell chimed. Still chuckling, Paloma headed toward the
sound. She opened the door, expecting a neighbor or FedEx,
anyone but a woman she couldn't place but vaguely recognized.
She stood there looking uncomfortable. Though she wore a
baseball cap, gray showed at her temples, and she had the deeply
weathered face of one who'd spent her life outdoors. Their high
school mascot was embroidered on the jacket of her track suit.

Paloma smiled. "Yes?"

The woman grinned, looking younger than Paloma had

initially thought. "Wow, Paloma Perea, you haven't changed a bit unless you count being more gorgeous than ever."

That voice! Her jaw dropped. No way! It was Deanne's old high school buddy in disguise as an actual grown-up. Reyna… Reyna…What's-her-face. That's it!

"Reyna!" She pushed the storm door open and stood aside. "Come in. I haven't seen you in, holy shit, years!"

Reyna removed her hat and smoothed long fingers through her flattened hair jock-style—once, twice, three times, front to back. "It has been a while, that's for sure."

Paloma pulled Reyna into a quick hug, then pulled away, curious about her sudden reappearance. Just seeing Reyna made Paloma want to don leg warmers and rip a sweatshirt so it hung off one shoulder. She felt like she'd stumbled back in time.

I'm a maaaaaniac, maaaaaniac…

"Deanne's running errands. You remember Iris Lujan and Emie Jaramillo, right?" She turned toward the breakfast nook without waiting for an answer. "Hey, you guys, come here."

They bustled through the archway, and Paloma couldn't help but notice that her friends didn't look nearly as surprised as she felt to see a life-sized high school flashback standing in the living room as if it was *normal*.

Iris strode forward. "Well whaddya know, it's Reyna What's-her-face." She shook Reyna's hand. "Good to see you."

Reyna chuckled, slanting Paloma a glance. "I forgot Paloma used to call me that. It's Falcon. Reyna *Falcon*." She nodded to Iris. "So, face-to-face with the most famous person from our graduating class. My wife has your *Cosmo* cover tucked in our yearbook."

"That's where I stuck mine, too." Iris deftly deflected the compliment with a casual toss of her hair. "I might be the most recognizable, but Emie's making a much bigger contribution to the world. She's a research scientist."

"That, I know. Hey, Em." Reyna offered a firm handshake. "In addition to coaching track at the high school, I teach AP science. Dr. Jaramillo speaks to my genetics students once a year." Reyna nodded to her belly. "I guess you're expecting a little clone of your own, huh?"

Emie beamed, her fists bracing her lower back. "And not a moment too soon."

"I hear you." She tugged the wallet from her back pocket and opened it to expose an accordion of photos featuring smiling brown children. "We've got seven. My wife carried four, I carried three. Round about the seventh month of each pregnancy, one or both of us fears for our lives."

"Seven!" Emie looked vaguely ill. "Reyna, you are speaking to a very pregnant woman, need I remind you. You should fear for your life right this minute."

Reyna feigned a terrified duck when Emie raised her fists, then provided names as Iris pawed through the proud mama snapshots.

Weirder by the minute.

Paloma cleared her throat. "A mama of seven is the perfect candidate for coffee." She inclined her head toward the kitchen. "Would you care to join us for a cup? Deanne should be home shortly."

"Ah, no. Thanks, but I'm due back at the school soon. It's my planning period." She stretched her neck from side to side, just as she'd always done before a meet. Mottled redness stung her cheeks. "I actually came to talk to you."

"Me?" Paloma tilted her face to the side. "What's up?"

Reyna cleared her throat, shooting an almost apologetic glance over her shoulder toward Emie and Iris. "Yeah, uh. Well, I was just, uh, wondering…" She chuckled, then shrugged, the grin tooling deep lines into her feminine-handsome, leathery cheeks. "Deanne wanted me to ask you if you might be interested in going to homecoming with her."

Ahhhh…huh?

The entire room and everything in it froze.

No one moved.

No one spoke.

No one drew a single breath.

Paloma felt like Samantha on *Bewitched* just after she did that nose thing, but Paloma knew, in her case, the magic couldn't last. She had to speak, to respond somehow.

Let's review: Deanne sent a pal to ask her out?

Finally, Paloma managed a half-choke, half-laugh, splaying a hand she couldn't feel on a chest that would surely explode if it expanded another millimeter. "You—you're kidding, right?"

Reyna clapped the baseball cap back on her head, settling it just so. "Nope. The dance is in two weeks, after the game, and I'm a freaking idiot who's always up for a dare, so this is your invite. Just like old times, eh?"

Paloma held up a finger, blinking rapidly and moving her mouth like a fish. "Let me get this straight. Homecoming."

"Yup."

"In two weeks."

"Bingo."

"And my partner of fourteen years enlisted your help in asking me out?"

"Uh-huh."

"For a date?"

"Exactly."

"To a *high school* homecoming?"

"That's about the gist of it." Reyna grinned. "Some things don't change."

"Oh, Pea." Iris jostled Paloma's shoulders. "It's the most romantic thing I've ever heard."

Paloma darted a dazed glance at Emie, the more sensible friend by a mile. But no. Em had her hands clasped at her chest and tears shining in her eyes. Paloma wanted to write it off to pregnancy hormones, but...she couldn't.

"So?" Reyna smoothed her palms together slowly. "Can I tell Deanne yes, or do you already have another date?"

Paloma's breath left her in a whoosh, and she sagged.

This was absurd.

Unheard of.

This was...this was...one of the sweetest things Deanne Vargas had ever done. Paloma's heart melted. "Of course I don't have another date, Reyna What's-her-face Falcon. I'm thirty-two years old, for God's sake."

"So, that's a yes?"

Paloma threaded her fingers into her hair and stared. This was so unexpected, she didn't have the proper words. After a moment, she made some ineffective nodlike motions with her head. "Hell, why not?" She laughed, feeling light and silly. "Tell Deanne I'd love to be her date."

Iris and Emie cheered.

Even Reyna looked triumphant. "Great." She turned to leave, then snapped her fingers and spun back. "Almost forgot. Deanne will pick you up at seven for dinner."

"Pick me up?" She frowned. "But Deanne lives here."

"Not that night. She wants it to be perfect."

Excitement tingled Paloma's flesh. "O-okay."

Reyna touched the bill of her cap and nodded to Iris and Emie before glancing back at Paloma. "One other thing. Deanne suggested you wear something red." Reyna looked ever so slightly lost. "I have no idea what this means, so don't hold me accountable if I've gotten it totally wrong. But apparently, red... is the new black?"

CHAPTER TEN

From Paloma Vargas's journal, homecoming night:

I haven't felt this excited about seeing Deanne in a long time. She dropped the boys at Emie and Gia's house yesterday to spend the weekend and packed a bag for herself. To stay with Ruben, I assume. In any case, she hasn't been around. This morning, however, I awoke to find a gift certificate for a spa day at a local salon tucked beneath a hot cappuccino. Sneaky.

Every time I think about it, my head swirls. It's truly like falling in love all over again.

So, now I've been massaged, salted, mud-packed, manicured, pedicured, waxed, and coiffed, and I feel like a queen awaiting the arrival of her royal court. Except in the most rudimentary way, Deanne and I haven't discussed tonight too much. It's been almost as if neither of us wanted to break the spell. And—holy hell—what a spell it is. The touch of mystery has only added to my anticipation. That and the fact that my new red dress fits like a dream and makes me feel utterly sexy. God bless stress for its slimming side effects. (Yoga and walking helped, too.)

I feel like we're on a threshold of a new beginning.

Deanne and I have weathered the storm. We still have work to do, but I feel like we can. Finally. I'm ready to put the past behind us and move on with our relationship.

Me <————hopeful. And in love.

I can't wait for her to arrive and take me to...I just have to laugh...homecoming. But only because that's one step closer to when she can actually take me home...

The doorbell rang, and Paloma's pulse kicked into overdrive. Oh, God. Moment of truth. Smoothing her moist palms against the ruby-red crushed silk covering her curves, she headed to the door and pulled it open.

Deanne.

In a coal black, utterly feminine suit over a light gray silk shirt, she looked edible, and Paloma? Starving. The deep open neck of Deanne's shirt offered an inviting peek at her cleavage—a good place to start the feast. A perfect red rosebud adorned her lapel, and the room felt suddenly more alive because she'd arrived.

Deanne's expression flashed with surprise and awe, then deepened into something feral as her gaze caressed Paloma's body like a Porsche hugging the open road. "Lord almighty, Paloma. If you've ever looked hotter, I can't remember."

Paloma's tummy flopped, and she actually had the urge to laugh. Instead, she backed up and spun slowly, treating Deanne to a full view of the dress she'd found only after trying about fifty others. All red. Did Dee have any idea how hard it was to find fifty goddamn red dresses in one city? "You like?"

"I love. Can I come in?"

She swept her arm aside. "It's your house."

"Yeah?" Deanne's expression was wistful as she reached out and trailed one finger just inside the edge of Paloma's neckline.

Paloma bit her lip, suddenly scared.

As though sensing her fear, Deanne entered the house, but stood away. A mischievous smile spread across her face, and Paloma noticed she had one hand behind her back.

Lighter tone.

Good choice.

She cleared her throat and lifted her chin toward the hand she couldn't see. "Whatcha got back there?"

"Something for you." Deanne rocked from heel to toe playfully.

"Hmm. A corsage?"

Dee frowned. "Damn, I knew I forgot something."

"That's okay." She tossed her trimmed and styled hair. "I wouldn't want to pin it on this dress anyway."

"Mmmmm, yes. That dress," Deanne drawled, her gaze as disreputable as her tone.

Paloma crossed her arms and watched Deanne look hungrily at her cleavage. Sometimes being a woman wanted by a woman felt more powerful than sorcery. "If not a corsage, then…wine?"

"Nope." Deanne's grin was wolfish and enticingly uncouth. "You think you'd be safe around me with wine on the menu? In that"—she swallowed tightly—"dress?"

Not in it for long. Paloma's chin lifted primly, but she bit her bottom lip to think for a moment. "Is it candy?"

"Silly to give candy to a woman as sweet as you." Deanne shook her head. "Three strikes. You're out."

Laughing, Paloma reached out. "Okay, sister. Give it up."

And suddenly, she held a plush white teddy bear wearing a miniature letter jacket. "Oh, Deanne! How absolutely cute…and silly."

Dee looked pleased with herself. "I would've worn mine, but it was too tight through the shoulders."

Paloma clutched the bear with both hands, grinning down into his black button eyes. "This looks exactly like the bear I wanted—"

"In eleventh grade, for Valentine's Day."

Her head shot up and her brows dipped. "How'd you remember?" Wait a minute. Deanne had been remembering a whole lot about high school lately. Paloma began to ponder this. "Tell me how you remembered."

Deanne feigned indignation, deftly sidestepping a straight answer. "Are you saying I have a poor memory?"

"You really wanna go there, D?" Her expression epitomized drollness.

Again, Deanne turned serious and almost predatory, but in a sensual, caring way. She reached out and cupped Paloma's waist, pulling their bodies together. Deanne's gaze traced the lines of her face, her chest, her mouth. "Nope. That's not where I want to go. Actually, I don't want to *go* anywhere. What I want to do is come home. *Really* come home."

Paloma's breath caught, and she knew nothing beyond the aching throb that had begun at her feminine core and the blinding need to feel Deanne's mouth on hers. This, *this* was how things felt between Deanne Vargas and Paloma Perea. *This fire* was what had burned them to trembling ashes the first six years of their marriage, what she'd missed so desperately since, what she wanted more than oxygen for her next breath. "I want that, too."

"You see this look on my face, Punkybean?" Deanne whispered, low and sexy. Rough. "This expression that says I want to be inside you? Now. Here. You see that?"

"Yes," she sighed.

"That's what your daddy saw that made him split us up that summer." Deanne bent forward and nipped Paloma's ear, pulling at her black pearl earring. Hot against her cheek, Deanne rumbled, "I wanted Daddy's baby girl. Wanted to see how fast I could get past her innocence and make her mine. Forever."

Paloma clutched Deanne's sleeve, leaning her head back to expose the rapid pulse in her throat to Dee's famished, urgent kisses. "D…"

A low, animal sound came from Deanne's throat as she

pulled aside the neckline of Paloma's dress and sucked on her exposed shoulder, warm and hot and wet.

Paloma's body pressed into Deanne's, and the teddy bear fell to the floor. Dee's confident hands smoothed over her back to her buttocks, cupping, claiming. "Keep this up and we'll never make it to the dance," Paloma murmured.

"Oh"—Deanne licked her collarbone—"we're going to make it to the dance." She hovered over Paloma, kissed the tops of her breasts exposed by the dress's plunging neckline "I'm just giving you something to think about"—her tongue traced Paloma's lips—"while we're stuck in that darkened gymnasium."

Deanne took her in a breath-stopping kiss, backing her slowly until she was pressed against the wall, but pulled away at the sound of her throaty laugh. "You laughed at me the first time I kissed you, too. What now?"

Paloma shook her head. "You are an evil, horrid tease. That's all."

"Wrong. I'm not teasing at all, baby girl." As if to prove it, Deanne thrust against her. Once, then again. "If you want the truth, we're only going to the dance so I can bring you home from it."

"Just like high school," Paloma groused lightly.

"Just like always, Punky. I want you something bad. I will never let you doubt that again."

Feeling weak and wet and shaky, Paloma pushed Deanne away. She might think they were headed to the dance, but if she kept talking against Paloma's skin in that stonewashed velvet tone, the only dancing they'd be doing was between the sheets.

Not that Paloma was complaining.

"Well, then, let me go fix my ruined lipstick, and we can leave."

She swiveled on her unfamiliar black stilettos and sauntered toward the hall, making sure Deanne caught every slow-motion sway.

"Whoooey. I need a swing like that in my backyard."

Paloma laughed over her shoulder. "You used to say that to me in high school!"

Deanne looked smug, and not at all surprised, Paloma noticed. Had they slipped into a time machine? If so, lock the door. She'd stay right here in the flames with Deanne, sizzling away.

The brash bathroom light slapped her with the present, illuminating her true colors. Swollen lips, drowsy eyes. She clapped her cheeks. Oh, God. She wanted her wife. Badly. Why couldn't she have a poker face when it came to Deanne Damn Vargas? As she re-applied the crimson color, she heard Deanne swear viciously from the living room. Warning tightened her chest, and she peered around the corner, down the hall. "What's wrong?"

Deanne didn't answer.

Paloma shrugged. Her imagination.

She blotted her lipstick on a tissue, fluffed her hair, and headed down the hall. "What are you swearing about?" Her eyes dropped to Deanne's hands...hands holding her work cell phone. She felt her world start to shred, her defenses drop into place. Warning screeched in her ears. *Don't say it!* "Deanne. What is it?"

Troubled brown eyes raised. "I got fucking mandatory paged."

Paloma's chest began to tremble. She crossed her arms, already feeling this magical moment, this magical woman, slipping away. "Don't call back."

Deanne flipped one hand over. "It's the emergency page, P. Mandatory. Not calling back is a firing offense. I should—" She cut herself off, pressing her lips in a thin line. "*Damnit.* Why this now?"

All Paloma could see, all she could feel was her precious dream crashing down around her. The pain ripped through her, worse this time. She knew she wouldn't survive it. "Are you going to call?"

Deanne remained silent, head hung, the muscle in her temple ticking.

"Deanne?"

Their eyes locked, gazes filled with pleading and pain. Desperation. Indecision.

Self-preservation flared, and Paloma threw her arms up. "Call work. Just go ahead. I never have been able to stop you."

"Baby, I don't have a choice."

Paloma stormed down the hall away from Deanne and slammed into their bedroom. Her hands shook with adrenaline and disappointment. She kicked out of her heels and paced the dark room from end to end, raging at the unfairness of it all. Yanking off her earrings, she tossed them on the dresser, gulping back a sob.

No. No crying.

She leaned her back against the door and closed her eyes. She was so stupid. *So* stupid. She should've seen this coming a mile off. Nothing had changed, nothing ever wou—

"Nora, hi. It's Deanne," Paloma heard her say. She stilled; her ears perked. "Listen...I got the page, but I can't come in. Whatever it is will have to—"

Deanne went dead silent, and Paloma couldn't help but crack the door and listen. Had she really told her supervisor she couldn't respond to a mandatory page?

"Jesus Christ, no. How the hell did that happen? Where?"

Deanne's voice had gone hoarse and shaky. Acid lurched in Paloma's gut. She knew that tone. As a cop's spouse, she *feared* that tone. She opened the door and stood in the hallway, staring down at Deanne whose back was to her. Her shoulders slumped with defeat.

"Oh, God. Not O'Doyle, too. His wife is just about ready to deliver twins." Deanne bit out a rough curse and slumped to a squat, swirling a palm over her head. "Where'd he take the bullets?"

Paloma's stomach plunged and stars rushed her eyes. A cop

had been hurt. No, a cop had been *shot*. A cop she knew, who worked Deanne's shift, who'd been to their house for barbecues and football parties.

It could've been Deanne.

As the room dimmed to a sickening black pinpoint, she grappled for the wall to steady herself.

Deanne's next words were strained, halting. Underlying those words, Paloma heard shame, futility, defeat. "Nora...you know what's been going on with me. If you can...get anyone else to cover—"

"Wait!" Paloma said.

This was wrong. Completely wrong.

Deanne shouldn't have to sound like that, to sacrifice like that.

Dee spun to face her, hope and fear and sorrow in her eyes.

With the sudden clarity of a roundhouse kick to the chest, Paloma realized how grossly unfair she was being to Deanne. Dee had done so much changing, made so many compromises. What had Paloma done to make things better between them? Jack shit, that's what. If she wanted Deanne to consider her feelings and needs, then she needed to reciprocate. And if Deanne had been one of the cops who'd taken the bullets, Paloma would damn well want every single one of her coworkers to drop their lives and rush to her aid. No questions asked. Shame threatened to choke her as she drooped under the realization and remorse about her selfishness.

"Hang on." Deanne cupped the receiver. "Paloma?"

"O'Doyle got shot?"

"Yeah. And Standish, who died on scene. And a couple of bystanders."

Paloma squeezed her eyes shut, gulping back nausea. "You have to go."

"No, P. Not if it means—"

"It doesn't." She closed the distance between them, pressing her palm against Deanne's cheek. "I…I have no right. You have to go, baby. I know that. I was scared and selfish."

Deanne's chest rose and fell a couple times, then she lifted the receiver. "Let me call you back in two minutes." A pause. "Yeah." She cut the connection.

"I'm so sorry," Paloma whispered.

"I won't go if it means losing you. I'm serious."

"Deanne, Officer Standish is dead." She choked on the word. "O'Doyle's wife is pregnant, and he's in danger, too. I've been unfair." She chewed her lip. "You have a life, other than us—"

"No." Deanne's head shook vehemently. "You are my life."

"I know. Honey, I know what you're saying, and I appreciate it." Her heart nearly breaking, she smiled and cupped Deanne's face in her hands. "I meant that you have other responsibilities. And I get it. I finally get it."

Tears sprung to Deanne's eyes and she started to tremble, clenching her fists to stave it off. "Goddamnit, Standish. I can't believe it."

"Go take care of them. His family. The other officers. O'Doyle." On tiptoe, she rained kisses on Deanne's lips. "I want you to."

Deanne pulled her closer and deepened the kiss, driving strong fingers up into the back of her hair. She took her like a desperate woman, breaths ragged and fast. Finally, she pulled away, both of them gasping for air. "We'll miss homecoming."

"No, we won't." Paloma rubbed her thumb over the nearly invisible scar on Deanne's chin from the fender bender. "You go be a cop, and we'll have homecoming right here when you're done."

Deanne stilled, eyes searching Paloma's. "You're sure?"

"I've never been more sure, Deanne Vargas. I love you, and nothing's gonna change that. I'll be right here waiting."

❖

The house loomed dark and still when Deanne headed wearily up the walk. She couldn't hold back the pang of disappointment, but it *was* late. Her heart ached over Standish and his family, but thank God, it looked like O'Doyle would recover in time to welcome his baby twins into the world. He'd been lucky, considering the bullet had entered his chest through the unprotected armhole of his Kevlar vest.

The case was huge, as one of the bystanders had also died from his injuries. Deanne couldn't help but feel grateful she was alive and coming home to her family.

She worked the key carefully into the deadbolt in case Paloma had drifted off. No sense waking her. Deanne felt certain they had all the time in the world to celebrate like she'd planned to tonight. Another night would have to do. Still…disappointing. She pushed the door open slowly, but to her surprise, the house wasn't dark. It was candlelit. Her eyes danced over the glow-softened interior before settling on the hand-lettered sign on the wall:

DEANNE VARGAS'S HOMECOMING
FOLLOW THE CHOCOLATES

A smile teased its way onto Deanne's face, and her heart began to pound with anticipation as she located the first Hershey's Kiss on the floor. She stooped to palm it, then noticed a second, and a third, a whole silver trail of them leading through the living room, into the breakfast nook—

Dee stopped short. Uh-oh. Clearly busted.

A circle of votive candles glowed and flickered on the table, and in the middle of them sat a red leather journal. A note on the front read, *You've read the rest, now read the best.* Deanne shook her head and laughed softly. She'd been so careful with that damned Cyndi Lauper journal. How could she have tripped herself up?

She popped a chocolate into her mouth and reached for the journal. The cover felt rich and smooth, and the color reminded her of the dress Paloma had worn earlier. A dress that had just begged to be ripped off. Deanne's body throbbed. She suppressed a shiver of raw need, opened the book, and began reading:

If you're reading this, then you've probably figured out that I know you read my journal. Thought you could slip one over on your wife, huh? Ha ha ha, silly woman. You must admit how unusual it looked when you suddenly started "remembering" stuff from the past. Memory has never been your strong point, you know (not mentioning missed anniversaries here). I put two and two together, then threatened Emie and Iris with their lives if they didn't confirm my suspicions. Don't you know best friends hold stuff over on each other for leverage in just such situations?

But don't worry. I'm not mad.

Me <——— totally reasonable woman.

Oh, my beloved Deanne…you know I didn't write those journals to keep anything from you, right? My journal was the one place I could always express my feelings without my mother telling me "good girls grin and bear it." I love her, I just don't want to live her life. Through writing, my true feelings always came out, as I'm sure you read. I only wish I would've realized I could express those emotions with you rather than on paper. Consider this the first entry in our journal. It turns me on thinking I can write whatever I want in here…to you. You can do the same. No secrets. I can't tell you how romantic it is that you'd go to so much trouble to win me back, Deanne.

Pat yourself on the back—it worked like a charm.

I've had a lot of time to think this evening, and I want you to know a few things. First, I love you. I want you back as my wife, my partner, my lover—forever. I have never wanted anyone other than you, and I'm sorry we've gone through so much lately.

But we survived, yeah?

Somehow deep inside me, I always knew we would.

I hate to think what might've happened if you hadn't been so annoyingly persistent.

I'm going to make you a couple of promises. I promise to be more open with you. I won't hold things in like I've always done. I promise I will never, ever make you choose between my love and your career again. That was unfair, and I will probably feel horrible about it for the rest of our lives. Keeping this relationship together isn't solely your responsibility. Know that. I'll work on myself, too, I promise.

I promise things won't ever get so silent in this house again, and I promise the past is the past. Ah, yes. You better also believe that I promise we'll never go six months without making love again.

On that note, I have a few promises I'd like you to make. Promise you'll always need me. And want me. Promise you'll always look at me in the way that'll make my daddy go for the shotgun. Promise we'll be together forever, Deanne Vargas, and that nothing will ever come between us again. Oh yes, please, for the love of God, promise you'll never play Rick James's Super Freak to warm me up. (ha ha)

And, Deanne? One last request...promise you'll grab the champagne from the fridge before you come into our bedroom. I told you I'd be waiting for you when you got home.

Well...you're home, lover.

And I'm waiting.

Emotion slammed Deanne in the chest. The words on these pages were written in the hand of a woman, not a girl anymore. Deanne adored both versions of Paloma, but this woman was her wife, and she always would be. Paloma loved her enough to give Deanne another chance. Her nostrils flared and her throat ached with pure, unadulterated love, as the words blurred before her eyes.

Deanne set the journal aside and crossed to the fridge. A cold bottle of Mumm champagne and a bowl of ripe strawberries occupied the bottom shelf. With a surge of desire, she retrieved them.

Knowing it would be a long, sweet ride, and not wanting one moment of it interrupted by the damn fire department kicking down their door, she took a moment to blow out all the candles on the table and in the living room. The delay was agonizing, but sometimes a sharp jab of pain was just the thing to bring a woman back to real life, back to the moment at hand.

Deanne crept down the hallway and eased open the door to find the bedroom blazing with candlelight, too. The air smelled of wax and woman. Her wife. The golden glow gilded Paloma's bare skin…skin barely covered by the red silk teddy and—*oh my sweet Jesus*—thigh-high hose. Deanne wanted to fall on the ground and weep with gratitude for being privy to such beauty. Instead, she moved to the edge of the bed and sat down. For a minute, they just stared at each other, warmth and love and forgiveness stretching between them, binding them in commitment forever.

Deanne reached out and toyed with Paloma's ring. "I promise," she whispered.

Paloma's chin quivered. She reached out. "Me, too."

With a groan of submission and possession, a love so strong it blocked out everything but this moment, Deanne swept Paloma into her arms and captured her mouth. She tasted both sweet and sultry, felt both familiar and completely new.

Paloma.

Her soul mate.

Thank God for second chances.

Pulling away, Deanne lost herself in Paloma's big brown eyes, swallowing back the knot in her throat. That familiar sweet ache filled her, and she said the only words that came to mind, the only appropriate statement for this moment.

"I love you, Paloma Vargas. Forever—"

"And a day?"

With a chuckle, Deanne shook her head, then slowly kissed her way down Paloma's lush body. "Not long enough, baby girl. Not nearly long enough."

About the Author

Lea Santos has been concocting tall tales since she was a child, according to her mother. Usually these had to do with where she was, who she was with, and whether or not she'd finished her math homework (which she hadn't). When it came time to pick a career, Lea waffled, then dabbled in everything from guiding tours in Europe, to police work, to bookkeeping for an exotic bird and reptile company—probably not the best choice, since (1) she never did finish that math, and (2) the Komodo dragons freaked her out. (A lot.) She eventually decided to go with her strengths and continue spinning wild stories, except this time, she'd turn them into whole books and call it a career. She rarely lies anymore about where she's been or who she was with…